Will Callie's dreams really come true...?

"He wants you on stage," Harry growled at her. "Go." He pushed her up the steps.

She stumbled at the top for there was no hand rail and the lights blinded her, but she regained her balance and walked toward Morgan. He had turned and stretched out his hand to her. She took it and stood beside him as he sang, "Share my North Carolina home? My Callie, oh, my Callie, will you share my mountain home?"

Callie looked into the eyes staring into hers. The two of them were in a world of their own, even though over five thousand people watched them, spellbound.

"Will you marry me?" he whispered, but his soft words carried over the North Carolina field and five thousand people held their breaths, waiting for her answer.

VEDA BOYD JONES writes romances "that confirm my own values." Jones lives with her husband, an architect, and three sons in the Ozarks of Missouri.

Books by Veda Boyd Jones

HEARTSONG PRESENTS
HP21—Gentles Persuasion
HP34—Under a Texas Sky
HP46—The Governor's Daughter
HP78—A Sign of Love

Callie's
Mountain

Veda Boyd Jones

Heartsong Presents

Dedication

To my sister, Elaine Jones, for always being there.

Acknowledgment

Thanks to Jimmie, Landon, Morgan, and Marshall,
who have taught me appreciation for different
forms of music.

A note from the Author:
I love to hear from my readers! You may write to me at the
following address:

> **Veda Boyd Jones**
> **Author Relations**
> **P.O. Box 719**
> **Uhrichsville, OH 44683**

ISBN 1-55748-633-6

CALLIE'S MOUNTAIN

PRINTED IN THE U.S.A.

prologue

Callie Duncan slipped her chemistry book on the lower shelf of the waitress station as the hostess ushered superstar Trey and an older man into the private dining room.

Callie was used to seeing celebrities. Actors, politicians, singers, and important businessmen often dined at Highridge House. But she wasn't prepared to see the famous singer, whose songs she sang along with on the radio. And Trey's tall good looks were even more impressive in person than on the cover of the *People* magazine her friend Sally had brought to school.

From the magazine stories Callie knew Trey's statistics: twenty-five years old, single, played the piano, and wrote his own songs. He'd graduated from Princeton when he was twenty-one and held a degree in business. He liked the color blue, chocolate ice cream, and watching late movies on TV.

Now, looking at the real live person, Callie took a deep breath and carried ice water and menus to the table. Part of her job training was to ignore celebrity status and treat all customers alike.

Morgan P. Rutherford III, alias Trey, looked around the small dining room and nodded with approval. No crowds of screaming girls had greeted him. No one approached him for an autograph. That was one of the many things he liked about Highridge, North Carolina. The local people were used to celebrities and respected their privacy, and the wealthy crowd who flocked to the Blue Ridge Mountains in the summer sought the peace of the mountains and escape from the demands of city life. None of them would interfere with another man's need for seclusion.

But sometimes the solitude that Morgan needed carried with it a burden that bordered on loneliness. He hoped that buying the house on Regal Mountain would make him a part of a group, without interfering with his need for a life away from reporters and screaming fans.

"Dad," he said, taking a sip of ice water, "I appreciate your coming with me today. I wanted another opinion about the house."

"Glad to do it," his father answered. "It's a great house. Wonderful view."

They ordered and were soon served excellent meals. Their conversation lapsed as they tackled their dinners.

"Victoria wants to come up," his dad said at last. "Your mom thought it would be fun to spend some time in the mountains, too. You may be getting more togetherness than you bargained on." He chuckled.

"I don't see enough of Vic and Adam and their kids. I want them thinking their Uncle Morgan is a guy who can give them piggyback rides and buy them ice cream cones. And somebody they can talk to when they need to confide in someone. Like I can with you."

"Like now?" the older man said with a lift of bushy eyebrows. "What's bothering you, son? I know you wanted me up here for more than my opinion on a house. You've bought two other houses without asking for my approval."

"I never could pull one on you, Dad." Morgan tapped his fingers on the table, glanced over at the waitress who was reading a book at her work station, then took another drink of coffee. "I need something more," he said in a low voice. "That sounds crazy, I know. I just bought my dream house on Regal Mountain, my new album hit platinum—and I'm not content."

Morgan set his coffee cup down with a thump. The waitress immediately appeared with the coffeepot in her hand. "More, sir?"

"Sorry, I didn't mean to put the cup down so hard. But since you're here, I could use half a cup." He smiled at the waitress, whose blonde hair was pulled back in a braid that almost reached her waist. She poured his coffee, topped off his dad's cup, and returned to her station in the corner of the room.

Morgan glanced at his watch. Just past eleven o'clock. He glanced over at the waitress, who had opened her book again. "Miss," he called, "are we keeping you?"

Callie looked up guiltily and swiftly made her way to his side. "I'm sorry. Would you like something else? More cream?"

"No, I meant should we go? Is the restaurant closed?" He was used to eating late so he could avoid crowds, but the girl looked too young to be kept up late.

"The kitchen is closed," she answered, "but you can stay as long as you want."

She looked him straight in the eyes, her gaze calm and level. She had to be seventeen or eighteen, he thought, an age that almost guaranteed that she knew who he was, and yet she didn't flutter her eyelashes or give him the coy looks that teenagers usually directed his way.

"What are you reading?" he asked her.

"Chemistry. I have a test tomorrow."

"Senior?"

She nodded. "Can I get you anything else?"

"No, thanks," Morgan answered.

She returned to her post and opened the book again.

"So, why are you discontent?" his father asked.

Morgan shook his head and held out both hands in an empty

gesture. "Maybe I got it all too easily. I didn't have to work for anything."

"Didn't you earn your grades in college?"

"Of course I did," Morgan answered, "but I didn't have to work at a job at the same time." He nodded toward the waitress. "She's just in high school and she's working."

His father glanced at the girl who appeared absorbed in her textbook. "You've worked hard at your music."

"Yes and no. The songs just came to me. If I hadn't had connections, that first album could have flopped." Morgan studied the fine linen tablecloth. He had no idea how to explain to his dad what he didn't understand himself. "I feel like I have everything, and maybe it's time to give some of it away."

"Away?"

Morgan looked at the ceiling for an answer. "I already give to charities. I tithe to the church. I know this sounds hackneyed, but I feel I should give some of the money I've made to those less fortunate."

"I've always been against that," his father said. "My philosophy is that God helps those who help themselves. I don't believe in giving money to others, but I believe in giving opportunity."

"How do you give opportunity? Give a job?"

"That's one way."

"Callie," a woman's high-pitched voice called. Morgan looked up as the hostess who had seated them entered the private dining room and approached the waitress. The teenager shut her book quickly, and her head lowered.

"Yes, Mrs. Allen," she answered in a small voice.

The hostess spoke in low tones that Morgan couldn't catch, but the girl looked chastised. She kept her eyes on the floor and nodded several times. She looked at his table, then looked quickly away.

Mrs. Allen walked to the table. "Would you like some dessert or more coffee, Trey?" she asked, using his professional name. His family had helped him think of it. One evening they had thrown stage names around, and Grandad had jokingly called his son, Morgan P. Rutherford the Second, by the name Deuce. It followed that Morgan P. Rutherford the Third would be called Trey. The name had stuck, and his adoring fans knew him by the single name.

"No, we're fine," Morgan answered. "Callie's taking good care of us." He smiled at the waitress who remained beside the work station, trying to reassure her that he didn't blame her for studying when she had a chance.

The hostess walked away with a final glance at Callie.

"Opportunity," Morgan mused, his mind going back to his dad's philosophy. "Callie," he called to the waitress.

She immediately approached the table with the coffeepot. Morgan placed his hand over his cup. "Callie, where are you going to school?"

"Highridge High School."

"And where are you going to college?"

She glanced at his dad as if looking for direction. "I'm not going to college," she said.

"Would you like to?" Morgan asked.

"Is this a trick question?" She laughed a humorless laugh. "Of course, I'd like to go."

"Where would you go if you could?"

"Probably University of North Carolina at Chapel Hill."

"Then you're going," Morgan said. "Someone who studies chemistry at every odd moment deserves an opportunity." He raised his eyebrows at his dad and saw the nod of approval. A glance at Callie showed her disbelief. But he had decided, and he felt good about his decision. Callie was going to

college. He would finance her education. Whether she suc-
ceeded or failed at college would be up to her, but she would
have the opportunity.

one

Callie reached for her phone. "Yes, Liz?"

"Morgan Rutherford to see you," the receptionist said in a breathless voice, her excitement vibrating across the intercom line.

"Send him in, please," Callie said calmly, although her heart pounded.

Why was Morgan Rutherford here at Brandon, Callender, and Clark's CPA offices? She fluffed her blonde hair, wishing she had a mirror. Except for last year when he hadn't come to the mountains, she had seen him each summer after the night five years ago that had changed her life.

In his elegant home on Regal Mountain that night they had filled out admission forms for college and gone over financial costs. They had met three times that summer to finalize her plans. Each summer after that she had met with him while she was home between summer school and the fall semester. They had discussed her schooling, but often the conversation had turned personal, and they had shared their innermost thoughts.

Morgan had told her how he disliked performing live, how stage fright nearly overwhelmed him. Callie had confided her fears that her grandma was aging too fast. In Callie's mind, they had become friends, even though they only saw each other once a year.

Still, she had been stunned when last year he had shown up unexpectedly for her college graduation. What a stir he had caused on campus. The news that he was in the dorm spread like wildfire, causing the dorm mother to call campus security to ensure his safety. That was a day from her wildest fantasies. When the afternoon graduation exercises were over, he had taken her for a long drive, and they had stopped for hamburgers at a drive-through place and gone on an impromptu picnic. Morgan had apologized for the simple meal, explaining that fans swamped him whenever he ate in public. She was practically stampeded when she got back to the dorm, and she hadn't seen him since.

And now he was back in Highridge. Was he out at Regal Mountain? Rumor had it that his family members used the home more often than he.

"Hi, Callie."

She looked up into the same blue eyes she had dreamed about for five years. His dark brown hair had a little gray around the temples, she was quick to notice, and his face had a few lines she didn't believe were there before, but he still had the same neat, athletic build. He was thirty now, but he would turn thirty-one on June twenty-ninth. Callie knew because she had read every scrap of information printed about her benefactor in the last five years, from *Who's Who* to the tabloids, although she only believed a fraction of what she read there.

She stood and held out her hand, and he took it in his larger one. "Callie Duncan, you've cut off your braid."

"Yes." She touched a hand to her cropped honey-wheat hair. Short hair had seemed more suitable for a certified public accountant. "Morgan, it's good to see you again. Are you staying awhile?" She motioned for him to sit down, but he waited until she had resumed her seat before sitting down in the overstuffed chair in front of her desk.

"I hope so. It's been a long time since I spent any time here in the mountains. I need the peace."

"I'm sorry about your father's death," she said, not knowing what to say next, but feeling she should comment on his loss.

"Thank you. And thanks for your card."

She had received a formally engraved thank-you note from the family a year ago, but she hadn't known if Morgan himself had seen the card. Now she was glad she'd sent it.

"How's your grandmother?" He sounded genuinely interested, not just passing the time with a person he saw once a year.

"She's not as spry as she once was, but she's getting around all right. You'd never guess her to be seventy-five."

Her grandmother's health was one reason Callie had once given up her dream of a college education. A broken hip had the older woman bedridden for the last month of Callie's senior year in high school. She couldn't go off and leave Grandma alone. But Morgan had hired a woman to stay with Grandma until she didn't need help anymore. He had seen to everything, and in Callie's eyes, he was a hero.

"I was hoping you could have lunch with me. Catch up on old times," he said.

Her heart pounded. This scenario had occurred in her fantasies countless times, but this was reality.

"Morgan, I'm sorry," she heard herself say. "I can't. I have a client coming any minute for a lunch meeting."

"Oh. Well, another time then," he said. He stood and flashed her his famous grin, then strode out of her office before Callie could say another word.

This was not the way things were supposed to happen. He should demand that she cancel her meeting and go with him. She didn't even know how long he would be in the mountains. Would he really come another time?

Liz darted into her office. "I thought I'd faint when I saw

him walk in. You never mentioned you knew Trey," she said, referring to Morgan by the name that appeared on his compact disc cases.

"There wasn't much to mention," Callie said. She had told only one person, Joe Lowery, that Morgan had put her through college, and that was because she and Joe had shared rides to school and had become close friends.

Grandma had looked on Morgan's financing her education not as a scholarship but as charity, and she had allowed Callie to accept the opportunity only with the stipulation that she pay back every cent when she could. Callie had agreed. Only last month she had sent Morgan the first payment in care of his company. Maybe that was why he'd looked her up.

"Trey is Morgan Rutherford," Liz said dreamily.

"The Third," Callie corrected. At Liz's questioning look, she elaborated. "His grandfather is Morgan Rutherford; his father was the Second; he's the Third."

"I have all his albums," Liz said. "When's his next one coming out?"

"I don't know. He writes all his own songs, so it takes awhile to produce an entire album." Callie admired his talent. His songs reflected his beliefs in tolerance and kindness to others. His music was popular, and he'd won four Grammys for his work.

"Trey hasn't given a concert in two years," Liz continued. "I saw him in Asheville four years ago. He's dynamite on stage. But you've seen him perform, haven't you?"

"Just on television, not in person. Listen, I need to finish this before Mike Warner shows up." She motioned at the report on her desk.

Liz walked out and Callie closed her eyes, remembering Trey in the last TV special she'd seen. He had sat at the piano and stared into the camera, looking especially at her, she'd thought, until the song ended and screams erupted from the packed auditorium. He reached for a rose from the bouquet on the piano and tossed one to a girl in the audience, blowing a kiss at the same time. That blown kiss was his trademark.

At that moment Callie had realized she wasn't the only girl to feel attracted to Trey. Except, she had rationalized, she knew the real Morgan Rutherford III. Or was Trey, the man who played the piano, sang in front of thousands, and blew kisses to teenage girls, the real Morgan Rutherford III?

᠈᠊

That night while washing dishes, Callie mentioned her benefactor to Grandma. "Morgan Rutherford's back in town. He asked me to lunch."

"Did you go, Callie Sue?" Grandma's voice was sharper than normal and Callie turned to look at her.

"No. I had a client coming in."

"Good. You know year-rounders and summer folk don't mix."

Callie had heard that phrase quoted to her since she was two years old. Normally she let it pass, but this time she needed answers.

"Grandma, why not?"

Grandma looked taken aback for a moment, then she picked up a plate and briskly rubbed it dry with a tea towel. "Summer folk are from a different world. They expect their money can buy about anything."

"I don't know about that. Look at Morgan. He put me through college. He changed our lives, Grandma." Callie pointed to the sink.

Grandma snorted. "We'd of done okay without running water."

Callie wanted to argue that. Their lives had been so much easier this past year, ever since she'd saved enough from her first few paychecks to afford the luxury of a hot shower, a real bathroom, and running water in the kitchen. Grandma had objected to spending all that money when they'd gotten along without indoor plumbing before, but Callie was adamant. Three years at the university had spoiled her and since she couldn't get Grandma to move, she spent her money making the old home place more comfortable.

Yes, the changes had helped their lives, but one look at Grandma's stony face told her arguing would do no good. She dropped the subject of Morgan P. Rutherford the Third, although in her heart she prayed he would come see her again.

ta

Two days later, Liz buzzed Callie.

"It's him," she said breathlessly. "Line three."

There was no need to wonder whom Liz referred to. "Hello, Morgan," Callie said, pushing the other button.

They exchanged pleasantries for a moment, and then Morgan said, "I was hoping you'd have dinner with me tonight."

Callie caught her breath. She wanted to go, but in her mind she saw Grandma's disapproving look. Why did she feel this deep-seated duty to honor Grandma's wishes?

"Morgan, I already have plans for this evening," she said. She did have plans. She was meeting with church members interested in the building project. But she could skip it, couldn't she?

"We'll try it another time," he said. "Good talking to you, Callie."

ta

As soon as she got home that night, Callie confronted Grandma. "Morgan asked me to dinner tonight."

Grandma looked sharply at Callie, but didn't say anything. Was that fear Callie saw in her eyes?

"I wanted to go, but I told him I had plans."

"Tonight's the meetin'."

"I know. And I'm going because I have the financial report. But I think I'll go if he ever asks me again."

Grandma's eyes narrowed. "Year-rounders and summer folk—"

"Don't mix," Callie finished. "I know. We're from different worlds. He hasn't asked me to marry him, Grandma." Callie looked away from her grandmother's eyes, because that particular event was a part of her wildest dreams, too. "He just wants to have dinner. Probably wants to see how his investment turned out."

Grandma dropped the spoon in the gravy, then fished it out with a fork. "Supper's ready. We'd better eat."

&

During the building meeting at the small church, Callie forced her mind away from Morgan and onto the leaking roof and structural repairs needed for the old church. An alternative was to build a metal building, like other churches around had done. At the moment her tiny church had little money, and what they had would have to be spent on stop-gap measures. The group decided to buy more tar for the roof.

Back at home, Grandma followed Callie to her room. She stood inside the doorway, fidgeting with the straps to her purse.

"What is it, Grandma? Is something wrong?" Callie asked.

The frown line between Grandma's eyes deepened, but she shook her head and walked into the other bedroom.

&

A week and a half later, Callie was working at her desk when Liz brought Morgan into her office.

"Callie," he said in a no-nonsense manner. "I just got back into town and found I'm to be at a surprise birthday barbecue for my mother's best friend. I hope you'll come with me."

He was back. She'd thought she would never hear from

him again. "You want me to go with you?" she repeated.

"Yes. When do you get off work?"

"At five."

"Good. By the time I pick up a present for Mary, you'll be off and we can go. All right?" He actually looked like it mattered to him whether she went or not.

"Is this a fancy party?" she asked.

"No. It's a surprise barbecue at my house. You look just fine as you are. I'm wearing this." He gestured to his khaki slacks and blue-striped oxford shirt. The long sleeves were rolled up to his elbows, showing bronzed skin.

"Yes, I'd like to go," she heard herself say. "But, I can drive there when I get off work. You don't have to pick me up."

"I'll be glad to follow you home," he offered. "Then you could ride to the mountain with me."

"Oh, no. Our road is a washboard after the spring rains, and a pickup is the only way to get in."

"All right. I'll leave word with Billy so you can come right up."

Billy's family had lived in the gatehouse at the foot of Regal Mountain as long as Callie could remember. His daughter had attended high school with her.

"I'll see you around five-thirty," Callie said.

"Good." He grinned, waved, and disappeared out the door.

Callie reached for the phone. Times like this, she was glad she'd talked Grandma into letting her have a phone installed in the old farmhouse.

Grandma didn't sound at all surprised that she was going out with Morgan P. Rutherford III—nor did she sound pleased about it.

"You remember he's summer folk and only here for a few weeks, Callie Sue. Year-rounders and summer folk don't mix."

Callie wasn't going to get into an argument about this. "Yes, Grandma, but he just got back into town and needs a date. I should be nice to him. After all, he did put me through school."

"Be careful, Callie Sue," Grandma warned.

"Yes, Grandma. I'll see you later." Callie hung up the receiver with a bit more force than was absolutely necessary. She and Grandma rarely disagreed, but sometimes she felt she was treated like a fifteen-year-old instead of a woman who had turned twenty-three in April. Of course, she thought ruefully, if she continued to take out her frustrations on inanimate objects like the telephone, Grandma could be justified in treating her like a child.

With determination, Callie tackled the report on her desk, updating figures on the Mangrum file. Thirty minutes later she tidied her desk and stopped in the ladies' room on her way out.

She looked passable, she decided. Usually she wore business-like suits to the office. Because she had no meetings today, though, she had chosen a simple pink seersucker dress and sandals. At least she wouldn't be overdressed for the barbecue.

She drove slowly out of Highridge, not for her old pickup's benefit but because the road curved, climbed, curved again, and then turned back on itself, and she was stuck behind a shiny new sports car. Year-rounders knew the curves by heart and could take them at a pretty good clip, but summer people usually traveled with more caution.

Nine miles out of Highridge, the gates of Regal Mountain appeared. Callie turned onto Regal Road and waved at Billy, who stuck a card in a slot which swung open the wrought iron gates.

The climb up the mountain was much steeper than the road from Highridge. Callie shifted to low as the road snaked upwards with one switchback curve after another. Trees crowded the edge of the road and hid the mountain houses from each other. The higher the house on the mountain, the better the view and the more prestigious the family. Morgan's mountain retreat was near the top.

Morgan came out the front door the moment she pulled into his drive. "Good timing," he called as she climbed out of the cab of the old pickup. He patted the hood as he walked by. "Have you had any trouble with her?"

"Not a bit. Grandpa bought it brand new when he sold some land next to the highway. He built the grandest shed for it and polished it every weekend. I haven't given it the kind of care he did, but we have always maintained it. Until I started to drive, it only had 8,000 miles on it. Now it's nearing 70,000. Grandpa and Grandma used to go to town twice a month, but I'm there every day of course. I hope to get a car of my own soon, but I've been putting my earnings into fixing up the house."

Suddenly aware of how she was rambling, she fell silent. "I'm sorry," she said after a moment. "I'm sure you're not interested in hearing all that."

"Nonsense. I enjoy hearing about you."

They walked back to his home, and he led her into the living room. The long glass wall drew her toward the deck. "The view here is so incredible."

"I never tire of it myself—but I thought someone from around here would find the view rather commonplace." He moved ahead of her and opened the french doors, then followed her out onto the deck.

"Not me. The pullovers on the highway are not as spectacular as this. Although Grandma owns Eagle Mountain, we live at the foot of it, in the valley. When my ancestors settled here, they wanted flat land they could farm, not a mountain that would produce nothing and was inaccessible in winter."

"Has your grandmother ever thought of selling it?" he asked. He had moved beside her and leaned on the redwood railing, looking across to where other mountains reared their lofty peaks.

"I don't think so. Our place is three miles off the highway on a dirt road. Just getting a decent road to the mountain would take quite an investment, so I don't think we'd have buyers beating down the door."

"I'd like to see Eagle Mountain sometime. How far is it from here?"

"As the crow files, probably two miles, but by road at least six. There's an old trail to it from this mountain that used to be used a lot for hiking. It's the peak to the right." She pointed, but she could tell he was looking toward the wrong one. "No. See the church steeple. It's hard to see because of all the trees. Now go to the second peak to the right," she instructed. "You've got it."

He had moved close to follow her explanation, his head beside hers as if to see through her eyes. His nearness had an unsettling effect on Callie. She had overcome her first anxiety at being with him because he had been so easy to talk to and acted truly interested in her background. But that was when he was at least three feet away. Now they were separated by mere inches. She could feel his breath on her cheek, smell the musky fragrance of his cologne, and she hoped he couldn't hear the loud beating of her heart.

She turned her head to look at him and found an odd searching look in his eyes. For a moment their gazes locked, and she felt he could see all the secret thoughts she'd had about him during the last five years.

The sound of childish laughter drifted up from below the

deck, and Callie looked over the railing but couldn't see anyone.

"The kids and Victoria are downstairs decorating," he explained as he escorted her through the dining room and into the kitchen, where Wanda the cook was preparing a salad. Wanda good-naturedly warned Morgan to stay away from the charcoal grill, and then Callie and Morgan took the back stairs down to the family room. Again one wall was glass, and the sliding door opened onto a patio at ground level.

"Callie, this is my little sister Victoria, who's been my nemesis since the day she was born."

"Not true," Victoria inserted, as he introduced his niece and nephews.

Callie repeated each name to get them in her mind and guessed at their ages. Jake had to be around eight, Angie could be five, and little Dave toddled around the two-year-old mark. Adam, Victoria's husband, would arrive next week.

"You have your hands full, Victoria," Callie said. Then she thought better of that statement. Victoria probably had a full-time nanny and a cook and a housekeeper. Callie had no idea how the rich really lived.

"You've got that right," Victoria said. "Davie's turned into quite a night owl, and it's wearing me out. He gets up from one to three in the morning. I think he's getting more teeth. Here, Jake, can you tie this balloon over there?" She handed her son the balloon and patted him on the back as he headed for the light above a round oak table.

"What can I do to help?" Callie asked.

"You and Morgan can string crepe paper across the room. Mom and Mary should be back soon, so we've got to get a move on."

Together Morgan and Callie measured, twisted, and taped metallic red and silver streamers from the light fixture to corners of the room, forming a canopy above the table.

"Thanks for inviting me to this party," Callie said. "When do the guests arrive?"

"We're here. It's just a small get-together. I wanted you to meet the family."

"I see," Callie murmured, but she didn't really see at all. Did he want them to meet her because he had paid for her schooling? She had hoped he was interested in her as a woman, not as an investment. But she had known that couldn't be true. They were from different worlds, just like Grandma always said.

"Morgan, I really appreciate your putting me through school. You rescued me from waiting tables all my life," she said as she handed Morgan a piece of tape.

"I'm glad I could help, but I don't want to be thanked again. We went through all this at your graduation."

"I know, but you changed my life."

"You changed your own life, Callie. I just provided the opportunity. By the way, what was the meaning of the check I received?" He pulled out his wallet, extracted her uncashed check, and held it out to her.

In an effort to make light of the moment, Callie stuck her hands behind her back. "I intend to pay you back."

Morgan looked at her and then at the check. "It was a scholarship. I give five scholarships a year now."

"Then you can apply the money to the next student."

Morgan carefully placed the check back in his wallet and stuffed it into his back pocket. "We'll see," he said.

two

Morgan could tell he'd said the wrong thing when he had offered Callie her check back. Even though she had stuck her hands behind her back in a gesture that reminded him of little Davie in a stubborn mood, she had drawn herself up to her full height, lifted her chin, and her eyes had challenged him to defy her decision.

He glanced at his sister and saw her interest focused on Callie. Vic had always been sweet and kind, the champion of the underdog. But when she was riled, look out. He realized he had just seen the same kind of look in Callie's eyes—and it wasn't one he wanted to face right now.

"We're through here. Let's check the barbecue," he suggested and opened the door onto the patio. The spicy aroma of barbecue filled his nostrils and despite Wanda's warnings, he lifted the lid of the charcoal cooker and checked the ribs, letting the heat out in the process.

Callie was looking over the grounds and again staring at the view. What was it about her that fascinated him so? He hadn't realized what that night five years ago would mean to him. It was the beginning of a satisfying feeling that he was making a difference in people's lives, but with Callie, it meant much more than that to him.

He had enjoyed the planning sessions with Callie when they had discussed her college career. The first time she had ended up spending most of the day, and he had told her things he hadn't told anyone else. She was a good listener. Instead of breaking into his monologue, she looked questioningly at him, silently urging him to go on. And he did. He told her of his reluctance to perform live. He didn't mind the recording studio, but being out in front of an audience scared him. If he forgot the words or sang off-key, he could not try again. He told her he was going to cut back on concerts, maybe stop them altogether.

"If you ask God, He'll help you do what you need to do." She stated her religious belief so simply and trustingly. Although he considered himself a Christian, he rarely talked about God to others. He tried to show his Christian belief through his actions, but in his line of work, religion wasn't mentioned much.

Since that summer day with Callie, he had prayed for help before each performance and had felt a guiding Hand from above. He still didn't like performing live, but the thought of singing in front of people no longer paralyzed him. He had Callie to thank for the new closeness he felt with God.

He glanced at her quickly, admiring the pale gleam of her hair. Once she had started school, she worked hard, taking heavy class loads each semester and going two summers as well. She wrote to him, in care of his house on Regal Mountain, telling him her plans, what classes she was taking, and sent him a grade report each semester. She graduated with honors at the end of three years.

At the end of each summer session she returned briefly to Highridge, and Morgan had made sure he was there to see her. She sent him a graduation announcement, but was obviously surprised when he showed up for the event. That was another day he wouldn't forget.

His impulsive visit to the university might have started as a lark, seeing how his first scholarship student had turned out, playing Professor Higgins to her Eliza Doolitle. But after seeing the metamorphosis of Callie Duncan, he was mesmerized.

Oh, he had seen the changes coming from summer to summer, but the young woman with an air of confidence he saw at graduation bore little resemblance to the nearly servile teenage girl he had met at the restaurant.

She was delighted that he had shown up; he saw that immediately. That the other coeds were so excited by his presence was part of it, he recognized, but he believed she had felt as much as he had that sharing her special moment of triumph had formed a bond between them. On that day, he was the listener and heard all her plans for her future.

He had wanted to see her last summer, but his father's death had kept him busy in Atlanta, sorting through papers, learning about the businesses from his grandfather, so that he hadn't made it to the mountains. But now that he was back, he intended to see her until he found out if that something special he had felt toward her still existed and why.

"Smells good," Callie said. "But didn't Wanda tell you. . ."

He cut her off by placing his finger to his lips, as if they were conspiring together, as he put the lid back on the cooker.

"Isn't it a bit early in the summer for your trip to the mountains?" Callie asked.

What could he say? Because he wanted to see her, see if he could get her out of his mind, he had rearranged his entire summer calendar. But if he said that, it would scare her for sure. When she wouldn't go out with him the first two times he'd asked, he'd retreated to Atlanta, but he had returned to try one more time. He'd decided if she refused this time, that would be the end of it. He wouldn't ask again.

"Yes, it's early. But I'm overdue for a long vacation this year. Last year I didn't get away at all, with all the details of taking over the office."

"So, you're in charge now? What about your grandfather?"

"He'd already handed over the reins to Dad, and he didn't

want them back. He said he knew I'd be ready to take over when the time came. Unfortunately it came too soon."

"What does this mean to your singing career?"

"I don't know. I need time to think about that. That's one of the reasons I came to the mountains. I can hire competent people to oversee the corporation." And he could. Even though his family owned six subsidiaries, from a retail chain to movie theaters to a small airline, he had top executives running each company. Did he want to be CEO and oversee the works—or hand that authority to someone else?

"But do you want to hand over your control?" she asked.

"I don't know," he repeated. "I'd like to talk it over with you."

"With me?" Her eyes widened as she looked straight into his eyes.

"Yes. You listen. You don't tell me what to do. Know what I mean?" He placed a hand on her shoulder.

She nodded. "Would it be something like graduation day when you listened to me decide which accounting firm to go to work for? The big one in Asheville or the smaller one here in Highridge. I knew all along I needed to come back and help Grandma, but I still had to walk through all the steps of the decision. You helped me to do that."

He nodded and smiled. She understood the pull they had for one another. She didn't treat him like a big star and bow down to his every wish. Other than the gratitude she felt about the scholarship, she treated him like a normal guy, which was what he was. A normal guy who was worth millions and whose name was a household word across the nation. Most people didn't see past the glitz to the real Morgan Rutherford.

"They're coming." Angie rushed out on the patio. "Grandma's back."

The group lined up behind the table, where Vic had placed

a large cake.

"Morgan, the piano," Vic said as she lit candles.

Morgan took his place at the upright piano and waited for his mother to bring Mary downstairs. The kids poked and shushed each other while they waited. Finally, Morgan heard footsteps on the stairs.

"I need to put these things in the family room," his mother's voice drifted down. "Thanks for carrying, Mary. I shouldn't have bought so much."

As soon as the two women appeared at the bottom of the stairs, Morgan struck up "Happy birthday to you," and Vic, Callie, and the kids sang along.

"For me?" Mary said.

Mary had lived next door to the Rutherfords in Atlanta as long as Morgan could remember and was an ex officio member of the family. She had never married, but had unofficially adopted Morgan and Vic. Whenever they were in trouble at home, they had escaped to Mary's house.

She blew out the candles, then turned to hug the kids.

"Morgan, when did you get back?" His mother kissed him on the cheek and demanded a bear hug in return.

"A couple of hours ago. Mom, this is Callie Duncan. Callie, this is my mother, Dorothy Rutherford."

"Hello, Mrs. Rutherford."

"Hi, Callie—and it's Dorothy. Mrs. Rutherford was my mother-in-law," she said and smiled.

Morgan was proud of his mother. She had been a tower of strength when his dad had died. Once he had discussed their marriage with his father, who admitted that a great deal of his success could be attributed to Dorothy. She was behind her husband every step of the way, loving him, admiring him, encouraging him. Her shrewd brain had been hidden behind his dad's forceful personality, but his dad had always listened to his wife's opinion in important decisions.

Morgan introduced Callie to Mary, and the group watched Mary open her presents. Mary opened the card on Morgan's gift and read it aloud. "Happiness always to the birthday gal. Morgan and Callie."

Callie glanced swiftly at Morgan, who sat beside her on the couch. "I knew you didn't have time to pick up a gift. Besides, you hadn't even met her then," he whispered.

"Thank you," Callie whispered. She watched the family joke around and was surprised when, before sitting down to the barbecued ribs, salad, and hot bread, they joined hands in prayer. This was not at all what she expected from Trey's family. But she'd learned five years ago that Morgan Rutherford III and Trey, the singer, were two separate identities for the same person. Something like Superman and Clark Kent. But unlike most people, she would equate Morgan to Superman and Trey to Clark Kent.

She enjoyed dinner. At first she smiled and said all the customary things, while the butterflies in her stomach danced wildly. But by the time dinner was over, she relaxed. Victoria obviously adored her older brother. Dorothy was as down to earth as Grandma. The older woman was not as polished as Morgan's mother, but Callie could see the same hard working, determined core in them both.

At one point when Dorothy and Callie sat by themselves, Dorothy mentioned her husband, and Callie murmured her sympathy at his death. Dorothy shrugged. "God has smiled on my life. I loved a wonderful man and he loved me. We had a joyous life together. And when I think of him, I smile. Oh, sometimes I miss him so much I sit down and cry my eyes out. But his motto was, 'If you're not enjoying life, you're doing something wrong.' So I keep going, trying to do the right thing. And I have his children, and that helps. Morgan is his father all over again. Vic has his fire, too." Dorothy was silent a moment, and then changed the subject.

ɔɕ

The next morning Callie climbed out of bed and walked over to the window. Another beautiful June day. As she padded to the small closet hidden by a printed cotton curtain, her mind was on the night before. She picked out a yellow skirt and a white short-sleeved cotton shirt. She'd change before Morgan picked her up for dinner. Tonight! She'd been surprised when he'd asked her, but then he'd mentioned earlier that he wanted to talk about his singing career. That he would confide in her thrilled her heart. Maybe there was a chance that he would see her for herself and not merely as his protege. Her happy mood continued through a quick shower, and she hummed to herself as she dressed. She fairly skipped into the kitchen.

"Morning, Grandma," she called to the wiry little woman standing in front of the wood-burning cook stove. "The coffee smells wonderful," she said as she poured herself a cup from the old percolator on the stove.

"You got in mighty late last night." Grandma frowned.

"Yes. It was a wonderful party," Callie said dreamily.

"Now don't you be gettin' high flyin' ideas, Callie Sue. Year-rounders and summer folk don't mix."

Callie nodded automatically, but she wasn't really listening. "Grandma, I have a date for dinner with Morgan tonight. He's going to pick me up here at seven-thirty. Please be nice to him. And I promise I'll remember that he's leaving in a few weeks. But there's nothing wrong with me seeing him while he's here. Nothing at all."

"Callie Sue, I just don't want to see you hurt," Grandma explained, her voice strained. She tapped the plastic spatula against the stove.

"I won't be. Is one egg for me?" She wanted to change the subject before Grandma got warmed up to her aversion that bordered on fanaticism.

"It is." Grandma scooped the eggs out of the iron skillet and onto two plates. Plucking two pieces of toast from the inside of the massive stove, she added those to the plates, dropping one slice in the process. She picked it up and put it back on the plate, then took her seat at the table, and the two women bowed their heads.

Instead of the usual grace, Grandma said, "Lord, please help me tell her what has to be said. Amen."

"Grandma, what's wrong?" Callie could see her grandmother was greatly disturbed.

"Lord knows I never wanted to tell you this, but I think you'd better know for your own good." Grandma fidgeted with the cup in front of her.

"Grandma, what is it?" Callie put down her fork and watched with growing alarm. Grandma hadn't looked this distressed since Grandpa had died.

"Callie Sue, you know your ma died when you was born. And we always told you that your pa was killed before that in an accident. Well, your pa wasn't killed. He just went away."

"Just went away?" Callie echoed.

"Daisy Lou was only seventeen when she died. So young." Grandma shook her head. "She got mixed up with a summer feller, and when he left it broke her heart. As soon as she found out she was pregnant, she wrote him, but he never came back."

"Grandma." Callie felt as if she'd been hit in the stomach. "Who was he?" she whispered.

"I don't know his full name. Daisy called him Phillip. She never would tell us his name, but on the day she died, the day you was born, she called his name over and over." Her eyes teared as she spoke of her only child. Grandma's other four children had been stillborn.

"Then my father is alive." Callie's thoughts muddled her mind. "Phillip," she repeated his name. "Phillip." With tortured eyes she looked at Grandma. "How old was he when he and my mother. . ." Her voice trailed off.

"He would've been a little older than her, probably twenty. I don't rightly know. I only seen him one time, in Highridge, and I didn't know then that Daisy Lou was seein' him." She snorted. "I ought to of known. I seen he was makin' eyes at her. Your ma was a real good lookin' girl, Callie Sue. You take after her," she added and patted Callie's hand.

"Did she love him?" Callie needed to know.

"Oh, yes, she loved him. She wouldn't tell Orie his name 'cause she was afraid he would of hurt him if he'd found him. And he probably would of. He was that mad."

"After I was born, did you try to find him then?" Callie had to know everything.

Grandma shook her head. "No, we didn't want to find him then. Daisy Lou was gone, and we was afraid he might try to take you away from us. I couldn't of stood that. You was all we had left of her."

"And he never tried to contact you?"

"Never. He never did," Grandma said and sniffed.

"What did he look like?"

"I only seen him that one time, like I said. I recall he was pretty tall, had dark hair. That's all I can say, 'cept I reckon he had eyes that pretty shade of green like yours. Daisy Lou had hazel eyes."

"How could they meet without you knowing?" Callie jumped up and began pacing the room.

"Daisy Lou cleaned house for a couple of families on Regal. She'd just walk over there on the trail. It's not far, under two miles. She must of met him there. She knew we wouldn't like her seein' any of them summer folk, so she snuck out at night to meet him. That's all she'd tell me about it." Grandma pushed out of her chair, walked around the table to where Callie stood, and put her arms around Callie's shoulders.

"Callie Sue, I only told you so you would know the danger in bein' with summer folk. It broke your ma's heart. Don't let the same thing happen to you." Grandma was crying.

Callie put her arms around Grandma and the two women, one stunned, dry-eyed, the other with tears running down her wrinkled cheeks, held each other in silent comfort.

Grandma pulled away and reached in the deep pocket of her large apron and pulled out a handkerchief. She dried her eyes and blew her nose.

"Callie Sue, you mean more to me than anyone on this earth. Please, please be careful of the summer folk." She replaced her hanky and began clearing the table.

Callie stood still, trying to evaluate all she'd heard. She watched Grandma carry their plates of eggs and toast to the new kitchen sink. Grandma, who never wasted food, tossed their breakfast in the garbage. "Grandma, I'm not going to break my date with Morgan for tonight. He put me through college. I owe him something, and he only wants to talk. That's fine by me. But it won't go any further than that. My mother was seventeen. I'm twenty-three. I know what I'm doing." She stepped over to Grandma and hugged her. "Trust me, Grandma," she pleaded.

"I do, honey." Grandma nodded and stuck her hands in the soapy dishwater. "The Lord knows I do."

"Good. I've got to get to work. Anything you need in town?" Callie asked as if the other subject was closed.

"No, honey." Grandma turned around and looked at her. "I'll see you this evenin'."

three

In a daze, Callie walked out to the pickup. Once inside, she lay her head on the steering wheel, all pretense gone out of her. Grandma was so upset, Callie couldn't show her true reaction to the startling revelation. She didn't even know her true feelings, just that she felt numb.

She started the pickup and drove by memory toward Highridge. Her mind whirled, sorting out the hurt and disbelief. She was illegitimate. For five miles her mind stuck on that thought.

"Dear God, help me handle this," she prayed aloud.

What were her parents like? She had never known them and had thought she never would. Now there was a possibility she could find her father. She had thought Grandma and Grandpa had adopted her after her mother had died. They had told her over and over that she was their little girl now, and of course her name was Duncan, just like theirs. Now she knew it was Duncan, not because they'd adopted her, but because her father hadn't married her mother and they didn't even know his name.

Did she want to find her father? He had deserted her mother, who had loved him enough to protect him from her pa's wrath. Maybe he had never received the letter; Callie tried to find an excuse for him. But what if he had just used her mother, discarded her as a summer fling, and turned his back on his responsibility as a father? What sort of man would do that? Did she want to meet a man who had disowned her?

She parked in her assigned spot at the office. During the

day she tried to focus on the numbers and statistics in front of her, but her mind kept wandering to her mother. When Callie was thirteen or fourteen, she had been curious about her, and Grandma had painted a glowing picture of Daisy Lou. But obviously that wasn't the whole truth. What had her mother felt when she had waited until her folks were asleep to slip out of the house and up the path to Regal Mountain to meet Phillip? Did he meet her half way? Did he take her places in a fancy car?

Her mind tossed out ideas, discarded them, and thought up new ones; but by the end of the day, she had accepted the idea that her father was still alive and that except for knowing that fact, she was still the same person she had been yesterday. The past could not change the type of person she was, she told herself as she headed the pickup back home. And she wasn't going to let it upset her.

She hadn't decided about searching for her father. She needed more time to think about that. For now she would heed the warning Grandma had given her. Morgan would be only a friend, which was exactly what he was anyway.

The sad part was, she had wanted him to be more. So far he had lived up to all the dreams she'd had of him during the five years since their first meeting. Was it fair to judge him by her father's behavior?

She had not resolved that argument when she turned into the rough drive up to her home. As the white clapboard house came into view, she felt a surge of pride that she'd been able to help Grandma fix up the house. With the fresh paint, she thought the house had a new air of cozy neatness.

She parked the pickup in the shed and walked slowly to the house, schooling her face so Grandma wouldn't see the anxiety that still lingered in her eyes. She tried to put the morning's revelation out of her head and turned her thoughts instead to the evening ahead.

Although she had warned Morgan about the three miles of gutted road that led to their house, he had insisted he would pick her up for their date. Despite the jumbled thoughts she had had about summer folk during the day, she couldn't stop her pulse from quickening at the thought of seeing him again. She sure hoped Grandma would be nice to him.

≈

Morgan turned the maroon van onto the dirt road that led to Callie's home. The van had a much higher wheel base than his sports car, and Callie had repeatedly cautioned him about her rough drive. The first few hundred yards weren't bad, but the road deteriorated quickly as it gradually climbed a gentle slope. He decided the rains must run right down the deep rut where the left tire should go. No drainage ditches lined the sides, so he hugged the right side and tried to dodge the largest potholes.

As he rounded a sweeping bend, the old farmhouse came into view. He stared at the homestead as he drove the remaining yards to the house. All that Callie had told him about the place her grandmother and grandfather had built together hadn't prepared him for the dilapidated structure.

The entire house had been newly painted white, but paint couldn't hide the decayed wood of the eaves and window ledges. Fieldstone piers struggled to hold up the sagging front porch. Two fieldstone chimneys, one at each end, towered over the one-and-a-half-story house, giving the impression of sentinels guarding the place. The house lacked any lawn at all, but was surrounded instead by bare rock and dirt, worn smooth, and the wild ground cover of vines and scrub brush.

He could see four outbuildings not far from the house and guessed one to be the garage Callie called the shed. He could see why. He had thought she was kidding when she'd told him they had gotten running water the year before, but the outhouse, the farthest out of the buildings, bore evidence that she had been serious.

At least half an acre was fenced off to the left of the house, and the garden rows inside were straight and perfect, early June peas climbing high on a hog wire fence, corn standing a foot high, and tomato plants lining one edge. Other plants he didn't recognize peeked out of the ground, all neatly weeded, obviously the vegetables that would feed the Duncans through the year.

Morgan climbed out of the van and walked up the slab stone steps to the front porch. Three rockers, their wood gray and splintery from exposure to the elements, sat surrounded by flowers in old coffee cans. Handmade pillows that would have been the envy of many mountain tourists lay in the seats of the chairs.

He knocked on the screen door and waited a moment before it was opened by a wiry little woman, gray hair fastened in a bun on the back of her head. Her face was lined from many years of hard work. She didn't smile as her piercing hazel eyes assessed him.

"How do you do?" Morgan said, offering his hand. "I'm Morgan Rutherford, here to see Callie." He wasn't sure she was going to shake hands, but at last, reluctantly, she put her small wrinkled hand in his larger one. Her grip was remarkably firm for such a frail-looking woman. Her small frame must have made him first think she was feeble, he realized, for he noticed now that her back was straight and she held her head high and proud.

"I know." She acknowledged his introduction without volunteering her own name. "I'll fetch her. Come in." Her tone was belligerent.

She held the screen open while he crossed the threshold,

then immediately left him and disappeared through a low doorway that led toward the back of the house. Since he had not been asked to sit, Morgan stood near the door, hands in the pockets of his gray slacks.

He looked around with interest. The room, shabby, with old furniture stuck here and there, was nevertheless immaculately clean and cozy. A large hand-braided rag rug covered most of the wooden floor. An old-fashioned sewing machine, with scraps of white fabric on the bench beside it, stood in one corner. A stone fireplace dominated the north wall, and on the mantle sat pictures of Callie, one of her grandmother and apparently her grandfather in their younger years, and a picture of another young girl who looked much like Callie.

He heard Callie's muffled tones before she appeared in the doorway. When she came into the room he couldn't hide the admiration he felt. She wore a plain white dress with short sleeves and a red belt that cinched her narrow waist. Her high heels were also red. She needed a halo to complete the picture, for she reminded him of an angel. On second thought, her golden honey hair could be her halo.

"Hello, Morgan." She said his name with that same soft quality he remembered from last night. Most people called him Trey, and it was refreshing to hear his own name from the lips of a beautiful young woman.

"Hi, Callie." He didn't know what to say. "You look wonderful. Pretty dress." The compliments sprang to his lips automatically, the deportment lessons from his childhood coming to his rescue. Not that he didn't mean them; she looked stunning.

"Thanks," she said and smiled. "Grandma just made this dress for me today."

Grandma had followed Callie into the living room and Morgan's gaze followed Callie's to rest on the pugnacious woman, her hostility toward him a tangible thing. Why she disliked him, he didn't know, but he did know he'd have to win her over if he ever hoped to know Callie better.

"You're very talented, Mrs. Duncan. Did you also make the pillows on the rockers?" He motioned toward the front porch.

"Yes."

"They're very nice. Do you display any of your work at the craft stores in Highridge?"

There was a pause, and Morgan could tell by the look in her eyes and the grim set to her mouth that he'd said something wrong.

"We don't have no need to sell stuff to summer folk," she said gruffly.

"I didn't mean to imply that you did, just that your workmanship is excellent." He could tell he was digging a bigger hole for himself. Callie bailed him out.

"Grandma's been sewing for me since I was a baby. She's taught me, but I can't hold a candle to her. Shall we go, Morgan? I'm famished." She picked up her purse and turned briefly to her grandmother. "I won't be late." She kissed the old woman on the cheek and gave her what looked to him like a reassuring look. Why would she be reassuring her grandmother?

Morgan wanted to take her hand, but he walked her to the van with a couple of feet separating them, since Mrs. Duncan's disapproving eyes watched him like a hawk. He felt as if he were sixteen and on his first date.

After he had helped Callie into the van and slid behind the wheel, he breathed a heavy sigh. "Is it me or the summer crowd in general?"

"You're very perceptive, Morgan," Callie answered, a quickly hidden flash of pain in her eyes. "It's what you represent." She hastily added, "I mean, in Grandma's eyes, you stand for all the summer people."

"Is there a reason why she distrusts us?" Morgan wanted to look at her to see her eyes again, but the rough road took all his attention as the van crawled along at ten miles an hour.

Callie was silent for so long he didn't know if she was going to answer or not. Finally, she said, "She had a bad experience with a summer person once and tends to hold a grudge. Isn't this road all that I promised?"

"That and some more. Are you going to get it fixed?" he asked, following her lead and sticking to a neutral subject.

"We've been working on it," she said shortly. After a moment, she added, "Sorry, I didn't mean to snap. It's hard work and I only have Saturdays. Grandma's a stickler for Sunday being a day of rest."

"I see," Morgan said, hiding his surprise that she had been working on the road herself. He had naturally assumed she would hire workmen to do such heavy work. He searched for another neutral topic and found one in the wild flowers growing profusely on each side of the so-called road.

"I understand there are more varieties of wild flowers here than in any other part of the United States. That's an odd shade of orange." He pointed to a species. "What's it called?" He knew he probably sounded like a tourist, but this was such a different Callie than the one he had seen last night, and he didn't know why.

She looked at him oddly. "I don't know the name. Are you interested in the wild flowers here? You hardly seem the type to traipse through the woods with a little notebook, cataloging flowers."

He chuckled at the picture she painted of him. "You're right. I'm not the type. But Mom enters the wild flower arranging contest each summer in Highridge."

"When did you start coming here? Do you have any relatives living here?"

"No, no relatives. That spring we met was when I bought the house. I'd visited an old friend, Robert Garrigan, the summer before."

"Robert Garrigan, the mystery writer?"

"He's from Atlanta. Lived around the corner from me when we were younger."

She seemed almost relieved at his information and the easy going Callie of the night before returned.

"Where are you taking me for dinner?" The sparkle was back in her eyes.

"I thought we'd go to Collett's. Do you like it?"

"I don't know. I've never eaten there."

"Never?" He was amazed. She had lived here all her life and never eaten at what he would have called the main eating establishment in Highridge.

"Never," she repeated. "Collett's, like two-thirds of the shops and restaurants in Highridge, is only open in the summer. Year-rounders could never support such an expensive place."

"I didn't realize so many of the places closed down." They had reached the main highway, and Morgan could glance at Callie now and again as the road, although curvy, didn't demand as much attention. He hesitated a moment, then said, "Do you hold a grudge against summer people, too?"

He knew he was treading on dangerous ground from the guarded look in her eyes. She had seemed comfortable with his family last night. What could have happened between then and now to change her attitude?

"No," she answered slowly. He thought that was all she would say, but she volunteered, "I don't even know the one Grandma dislikes so."

"Someone I might know?" He was prying, but he was curious about the person whose past he was going to have to overcome.

She was silent for over a mile. "His name is Phillip," she said in a small voice. "I don't know his last name."

Morgan had hurt her, and he didn't know how. But he didn't want to hear that tone of voice ever again. "I don't know any Phillip on Regal Mountain," he said and grimaced, thinking he would sure like to know him. In fact, he'd like to find out what this was all about so he could make sure this Phillip could never hurt her again.

"Vic wants to see you again," he remarked, changing the subject once more. "She's only here another week before her husband joins her and the kids, and then they take off for Maine to visit his family. Could you come to the house for dinner next week?"

"Sure. I like your sister and her kids."

"They're a handful, but fun, happy kids."

They discussed the safe topic of his family until they arrived at Collett's and were ushered to a table beside the open-air balcony that ran along Main Street. French doors closed out the cool night air. The restaurant wasn't full, since it was still early in the season for the summer crowd. By the end of June, the place would be booming, and booking a table at the last minute would be impossible, even if his name was Trey. Then the balcony would be the most popular spot in Highridge.

Morgan was relieved to see no teenagers in the room, which assured them a peaceful dinner without autograph seekers. His older fans rarely approached him, and only at the beginning of the summer season was he hounded in Highridge. Once teenagers got used to seeing him in the restaurants and on the street, except for the brashest ones, they usually left him alone.

After they studied the menu, Morgan ordered for both of them. No sooner had the waiter disappeared, than he reappeared with water glasses and a stuffed artichoke salad.

"The movie house is busy," Callie said. She motioned toward the windows where the theater across the street was visible through the balcony railing.

"I wonder what's playing," Morgan said. "Back home you can go see any movie you want, any night, and yet I rarely do. Here, with only one movie theater, it's exciting to go."

"I know what you mean. At Chapel Hill we had several theaters, but it wasn't the thrill it is here, waiting for a special movie to finally come."

"Tell me about the university, Callie. What was it like for you in Chapel Hill?"

"I was scared at first. Although it was a dream of mine for a long, long time, I had always thought I couldn't go because of the expense. And when I finally got there, because of you . . ."

"Whoa," he interrupted as he heard gratitude in her voice. "Forget the financial part of it. We agreed we wouldn't speak of it again. I want to know how you liked it, what you did." They hadn't had time to discuss those years at her graduation.

"I was terribly homesick at first. I wanted to come home for Thanksgiving, but it was too expensive. I did get to come home over semester break at Christmas. I found an ad on the bulletin board. A student from Franklin needed someone to share gas with him. From then on, when he came home, I had a ride."

"Do you still see him?"

"Once in a while. We were both fortunate to get jobs back in this area. Joe works in a bank in Franklin."

"Did you date while you were in school?" What a stupid

question. Of course she dated. What did he expect?

"Yes, I went out," she said and laughed. "How else would I get to go to the movies?"

"You mean you used men just to go to the movies?" he teased.

"No. I was very selective and only went out with the ones I liked. I only use men to get steak dinners," she said solemnly as their steaks were set down in front of them.

She winked and Morgan laughed out loud. After a stale recording studio, she was a breath of fresh air.

four

"Grandma, he's just coming over to help with the road," Callie explained. "No harm in that is there? Morgan's just being neighborly."

"Neighborly?" Grandma snorted. "We got good neighbors, and they ain't that close-knit bunch on Regal. I doubt you'd see them being neighborly to year-rounders."

Callie ignored Grandma's jab at Regal. What could she say anyway? Regal Mountain was known as an exclusive and closed society.

"I mentioned we've been working on the road on Saturday afternoons, and he said he'd come over and help. I couldn't tell him not to come since he offered. It's not like I asked him to help us. Besides, Grandma," Callie added, trying to persuade the woman to her point of view, "he's a man and a lot stronger than us. He'll be good labor."

"Humph. He's comin' over here just to see you again. I don't want you hurt, Callie Sue.

"I'm not going to get hurt," Callie protested. "He's probably only going to be in Highridge a couple of weeks longer anyway. He'll be gone before you know it."

She turned back to the noon meal dishes, not waiting for a reply from her grandmother. Grandma was right, of course. Morgan *was* coming over to see her. And she was glad. He had done nothing to disillusion her five years of dreaming about him. He was kind, sensitive, strong, had a great sense of humor, and he seemed to like her, too.

She wouldn't get hurt. She knew it was only a summer

friendship, if friendship is what it could be called. He had kissed her last night—and it wasn't a kiss of friendship, but the kiss between two adults who were drawn to each other. She closed her eyes, remembering how he had walked her to the front door, his arm draped around her shoulder. Before he said goodbye, he had pulled her to him in a warm embrace, leaning down to kiss her ever so gently and lingeringly.

"Callie Sue?"

She opened her eyes and realized she was still washing the same plate she had picked up a full minute earlier. "Yes, Grandma?" she answered guiltily.

Grandma stared hard at her for a moment, then said, "Nothin'," and walked into the other room, muttering under her breath.

Callie washed the rest of the dishes and scurried outside where Grandma was already getting tools out of the workshop.

"You reckon he'll bring any tools with him?" Grandma asked. "Maybe a big ol' road grader?"

Callie chuckled. If Grandma could tease about him, even if it was about his money, maybe she was beginning to soften a bit.

"I doubt if he'll bring anything," she answered. "Except muscles and we can sure use those."

They walked a hundred feet down the drive and set to work, one on each side of the one-car lane. In places grass grew up between the paths of the tires.

Callie pushed the shovel into the soft ground beside the road and carried the dirt to the closest rut. While she worked, her mind jumped back to last night and her conversation with Morgan. Although she had tried to block it out, her parentage had continued to occupy a great deal of her thoughts, and she had been greatly relieved to discover that he had never had relatives on Regal. Therefore, they couldn't be related. That had been part of her fears when Grandma had told her about her father.

She decided that since she had never known her father, whether he was dead or alive didn't matter. He hadn't been there during her childhood, and she didn't need him now.

As her thoughts circled in her mind, her body worked with the shovel. After fifteen minutes of filling holes, her shoulders ached.

"No wonder we don't make much headway, Grandma," she pointed out, noticing that Grandma was also leaning on her shovel. "We tire out too fast."

At the sound of a car engine coming slowly down the lane, they turned their heads and watched Morgan maneuver the maroon van to a standstill a few yards past where they were working. He climbed out of the van, wearing worn blue jeans and a white tee-shirt that stretched across his wide chest. His clear blue eyes assessed the situation.

"Good afternoon, Mrs. Duncan, Callie," he called.

"Hello, Morgan," Callie answered.

Grandma merely nodded.

He slammed the van door and walked toward Callie and took the shovel out of her hands. "How exactly are you tackling this road?" He got straight to the point, not mincing words with pleasantries.

"We're just shoveling dirt into the holes," Callie said and shrugged.

"I see." He turned back toward the house and traced the road with his gaze. "When it rains, this road becomes a river, doesn't it?" He addressed Grandma, since her shrewd eyes had been watching his every move.

"It does."

"Well, then," he said, "it seems to me you need a drainage

ditch on each side of the road. Otherwise, you'll be doing this every year as the spring rains wash out new ruts."

Callie exchanged glances with Grandma. "We do fix the worst of it every year. Although it's really deteriorated fast since it's just been Grandma and me."

In silence, Morgan walked to the side of the road and down a hundred yards or so, then back up to the women. "It appears there was a ditch of sorts here some time ago, but it's filled in over the years. See the sunken area over here," he said and pointed to a grassy area two feet from the edge of the road.

Again Callie and Grandma exchanged looks. "I reckon there did used to be one there," Grandma admitted, a touch of respect in her voice. "Orie always took care of the road afore he died. Callie Sue and me let it go for a couple of years, then started fillin' in the chuck-holes. I never thought about that ditch."

"I didn't either, Grandma," Callie hurried to add, knowing Grandma was mentally whipping herself for not seeing the obvious. "And while I was in Chapel Hill, the lane didn't get much use, so it just got worse."

"I'll work from the yard toward you," Morgan said. "Callie, get the dirt to fill the ruts from a straight line like this." He drew a line with the shovel along the side of the lane. He handed the tool back to Callie. "Mrs. Duncan, do you have a pick?"

"Yep. In the workshop." She started in that direction, but Morgan stopped her, placing a hand on her shoulder.

"I'll get it. Second building?" He pointed to a shed.

"Yep."

Morgan set off for the workshop, and Callie and Grandma started work again.

"Can't believe I didn't think about that ditch," Grandma mumbled to herself. "Summer folk tellin' me how to get water to run off. What a day!"

What a day, Callie echoed in her mind, when Morgan returned. He had assumed command of the road gang, and although he worked three hundred feet away from them, he was still in charge.

After a half hour of hard labor, Morgan called, "Mrs. Duncan, do you think we could have a cool drink in a few minutes?"

Grandma went into the house while Callie and Morgan worked on. The day was not hot, the temperature probably only in the mid-seventies, but Callie could feel the sweat on her forehead and down the middle of her back. Moving dirt was back-breaking labor.

"Bring your shovel up here," Morgan called. He showed her where to put the dirt he had loosened with the pick, having dug down about six inches and across about a foot. "We don't need a wide ditch, just enough for the water to run off."

He had a fine sheen on his face from his exertion, but he kept up a steady rhythm with the pick as if he was accustomed to manual labor, though Callie knew he was more at home behind a microphone in a recording studio—or lately behind a desk in the corporation headquarters.

"This is going to take forever. How far does your land extend, Callie?" Morgan took a handkerchief out of his hip pocket and rubbed his face.

"The county road dead ends into our lane, so it's hard to tell the difference. We have about a quarter of a mile. But the county road hasn't been maintained in years. There are only three houses on it, and we're the only one for the last two miles, so I guess other roads with more use get the county money."

"Hmmm. Your grandmother's on the porch. Let's take a break."

They laid down their tools and walked up to take their places in the rocking chairs and drink the ice water Grandma had brought out in a tin pitcher. Morgan drank three glasses before the trio marched back to the lane. This time they worked closely together, Morgan loosening the dirt with the pick, Grandma and Callie shoveling it into the potholes.

After another half an hour Morgan asked Grandma to bring out more water. "She shouldn't be out here doing this kind of work," he told Callie when Grandma was out of ear shot.

"I know, but I'm not going to tell her that." Callie smiled. "She knows her limits, but she'll work hard until she gets there."

"Can you think of something else for her to do?"

"Will you stay for supper? I'll ask her to fry some chicken and fix a big meal. That'll keep her busy. How about an apple pie? That she can start baking now."

"I'll stay. Can't resist apple pie." He laughed.

Callie scurried off to inform Grandma that Morgan would be staying for dinner. When Callie returned with the glass of water for Morgan, he casually rested one arm around her shoulders as he drank. His touch sent her senses reeling, but all too soon he finished his drink and withdrew his arm as he handed her back the glass.

The rest of the afternoon he worked tirelessly. Callie couldn't keep up with him, so he alternated between the pick and the shovel. At the end of the day, they had completed only a fourth of the lane, but Callie was more than satisfied with their work. She was exhausted, but after washing up, Morgan looked as fresh as when he'd started.

"Aren't you tired?" she asked. She stood in the living room and pushed her elbows behind her to ease her aching back muscles. "You worked circles around me, and I'm about to drop."

Morgan knew that his muscles would scream at him tomorrow, but he didn't admit it. "Right now all I can think about is that apple pie you promised. It smells wonderful in here."

"Come and get it," Grandma's voice carried into the living room.

When they were all seated, Grandma asked Morgan to say grace. Without missing a beat, he held out his hands to take Grandma's and Callie's hands. "Father, thank You for this day. And thank You for the food we are about to receive and for the good woman who has prepared it for us. Amen."

Callie felt a squeeze from Grandma's hand and glanced at her. The older woman had a puzzled look on her face, as if she didn't know what to believe.

Grandma had fixed enough to feed half a dozen, but Morgan did justice to the meal, and Grandma had a self-satisfied smile as she watched the big man heap thirds of mashed potatoes and gravy, fried chicken, fresh biscuits, and fresh green onions and radishes on his plate.

"Excellent meal, Mrs. Duncan," he complimented Grandma.

"Them onions and radishes are the first of this year's crop," she said proudly.

"I noticed your garden last night. Looks like it belongs in a magazine," Morgan observed.

Grandma flowered under his praise. "Well, I do take good care of it. After all, it feeds us all year. I can most everything. The apples in the pie are from last fall."

"I didn't notice an orchard."

"It's around back. I'll show you," she said, then bit her lip, as though taken aback by her own offer.

"Why don't you both walk around while I start on these dishes," Callie said. "We can have dessert on the porch in a few minutes."

"Good idea," Morgan hastily agreed, getting up from the table. "I need to walk off this meal before I start on apple pie." He pulled out Grandma's chair and walked her to the back door. "Be back soon." He winked at Callie.

Grandma looked disgusted, as if she'd been taken in, but with her head held high, she walked out the back door that Morgan held open for her.

&

The next morning as Callie drove the old pickup down the lane, she said, "Look how far we got yesterday. Without Morgan, we wouldn't have gotten nearly that much done."

Grandma grunted, "He helped."

At Sunday School, Callie stood and gave the financial report. The Sunday School president, who had been at the building meeting, organized a work day to tar the roof.

"We've got to decide on a way to raise money," the elderly man said. "We won't be able to build a new church for fifty years if we don't come up with some way to bring in the dollars. Since we got a preacher this week, we won't spend time on it now. But next week, we've got to make some decisions."

He sat down and let the biweekly preacher take the pulpit. "Worry is not for the Christian soul," the preacher began. "James Russell Lowell said, 'The misfortunes hardest to bear are those which never happen.' And Luke said in chapter 21, verse 34, 'Be careful, or your hearts will be weighed down with. . .the anxieties of life. . . .' Worry is futile. We should be free from concern. We should face life's troubles as they come and turn them over to God."

Face life's troubles as they come, thought Callie, and turn them over to God. She didn't hear the rest of the sermon. Instead she talked silently with God, telling Him of her worry about not knowing who her father was, her worry about

Grandma not liking Morgan, and her worry that her feelings for Morgan were not returned.

By the time the small congregation stood for the closing hymn, she felt a great burden lift from her shoulders.

five

"Good morning, Vic." Morgan greeted his sister with a lazy smile. "Is there plenty of coffee?"

Vic poured him a cup and sat down with one of her own at the kitchen table. "What are you up to this fine Monday morning, Morgan? Do you have to work?"

"I was just about to ask you the same question. Where are the kids?" He took a sip of the hot brew and set down his cup as Wanda came in.

"Hot muffin, Morgan?" the cook offered, pulling a tray of delicious smelling muffins from the oven.

He sniffed. "Blueberry?"

"Of course. I know your favorite."

"You're too good to me, Wanda." He buttered two of the steaming muffins.

"I know it, and don't you be forgetting it either."

Dorothy entered the kitchen. She reached for a cup of coffee, then looked over her shoulder at Morgan. "How was your visit with Callie? You never mentioned it yesterday."

"So that's where you were Saturday night." Vic's eyes sparkled with curiosity. "I thought you were over at Robert's."

"I had dinner with Callie and her grandmother. We worked on smoothing out their drive, and I thought I'd go back over today and do a little more."

Victoria laughed. "I do believe you've met your match, Morgan, if she can get you out leveling a gravel drive."

"I didn't say it was gravel. In fact, it's a dirt drive. I'm digging a drainage ditch along side it." He knew he was letting himself in for it, but he wanted Vic's help.

"This is better than I thought," she said and giggled. "The Grammy-award-winning singer and new CEO of the Rutherford Group digging ditches to impress his love."

"I think it's quite admirable," Dorothy said. Morgan saw a knowing look in her eyes.

"Thanks, Mom. Now, Vic, I thought we could take the kids over to Callie's and work on the lane awhile. Have a picnic."

"No fooling? Okay, why not? The kids are still in bed, but it won't take them long to get around."

"No hurry. I need to make a few calls and run into Highridge on an errand. We'll leave here around ten-thirty. Pack a good lunch, Vic."

Morgan carried his coffee cup with him to the study and called the office in Atlanta. He spoke briefly to his secretary, then was transferred to Charlie Lockard, his right hand man. Morgan consulted his list on a yellow legal pad and jotted down notes beside each item. In concise terms, he directed Lockard, crossing some items out, adding more to the bottom of the list.

"Keep me posted on the contract renegotiations with the airline attendants, Charlie. I'll be out the rest of the day, but you can leave a message. Switch me back to Rochelle, please."

He dictated three letters to his secretary and asked her to collect more data on two of the new items on his legal pad. Making choices was difficult enough without meeting the people involved. He needed every scrap of available information that would help him make the best decision.

"Your manager has called twice. I told him I'd be talking to you, but I didn't tell him you were in the mountains. Don't be surprised if he doesn't call there next, though. He's pushy."

"That's why he's a good manager," Morgan said. "I'll call him." He didn't want to talk to Harry Caywood, though.

Morgan didn't know what he was going to say. He had a corporation to run—and he had a singing career to promote. Or did he?

He hadn't talked to Callie about it the way he had planned. The evening they had gone out to dinner, she had seemed troubled, and he didn't want to bring up his own problems. He'd given his future plenty of thought, but he had a feeling that talking it out with Callie would help him put everything in perspective.

With reluctance he picked up the receiver and pushed Harry's programmed number. He didn't like what he heard. He'd been asked to star in the Super Bowl half-time show. It wasn't even football season, but the show had to be lined up.

"I'll call you in a few days with my decision," he told Harry, but his initial reaction was to say no.

"What's to decide? We're talking the Super Bowl. You know how many millions watch that? You've got to do it, Trey. It's been too long since you've been on tour. You need the exposure."

"I'll consider it and call you by Wednesday," Morgan assured his manager before hanging up.

A frown line remained etched on his forehead, but Morgan was pleased with how quickly he had finished his morning's work. He rewarded himself by taking another muffin with him as he cut through the kitchen on the way to the garage.

He drove straight for Pressman's Grocery Store. He could have called Darrell Pressman, but some things were better done in person. He took Darrell out for coffee and explained the county's negligence in caring for the road that led to Eagle Mountain.

Darrell, the sixty-odd-year-old grocer and county commissioner, was receptive, even ingratiating. Morgan might have felt a twinge of guilt at using his position as a wealthy taxpayer in the county to persuade a county commissioner to get that road fixed, but on this issue he felt vindicated because of the years of neglect.

After delivering Darrell back to his place of business, Morgan swung his car onto the highway and headed back to Regal Mountain. He felt another twinge of guilt at his plan to win Callie's grandmother. After yesterday's walk to the orchard, if all went according to his expectations, today might harvest even greater rewards. Callie was no fool, and she knew what he was doing. She'd seen right through him, but she had seemed pleased.

Vic and the kids were ready when he arrived back at his mountain home. They piled into the van amid laughter and kidding that continued until they reached Callie's turnoff. As he maneuvered the van down the difficult road, Morgan called for quiet and explained the situation. He impressed upon the kids that they were to be extra polite to Mrs. Duncan.

Callie's grandmother was in the garden when Morgan brought the van to a halt. He directed the others to stay in the van until she had given them permission to have their picnic.

As Morgan walked toward her, she straightened up, her pose one of questioning mistrust. Surely, Morgan thought, yesterday's work had made some headway with her.

"Good morning, Mrs. Duncan." Morgan didn't wait for her greeting, but continued, "I was hoping you wouldn't mind if I worked on the lane a bit more. I brought helpers today. My niece and nephews need some planned activity," he said as if confiding in her. "I thought a little shoveling would use some of their energy and make sure they were tired enough for a good night's sleep." He added for good measure, "I'm baby-sitting tonight." The idea had just occurred to him, but he thought it was a good one. Vic would be glad for a night off.

Mrs. Duncan smiled. "Young uns can sure wear a person

out if you don't beat them to it."

"Then you don't object to us working on the road?"

"Nah. But tell me, Morgan," his ears pricked up at her use of his given name, "you out to impress my Callie Sue?"

"Yes, ma'am, I surely am," Morgan said and grinned. He waved for the troops to unload.

Morgan introduced his sister and the kids, then took them to the workshop for tools. They made a curious parade, him leading the way, Victoria behind, the children following, each shouldering a tool. Even little Davie carried a tiny spade that Mrs. Duncan must use for repotting flowers.

After fifteen minutes of concentrated effort, Davie and Angie deserted to play in the shade of a tree. Jake manfully did his best to keep up with Morgan and Vic. When at last Jake left them to find out what his sister and brother were up to, Morgan told Vic that he'd watch the kids so she could take their mom out to dinner. As he figured, Vic didn't refuse the offer.

Lunch was a festive occasion. Wanda and Victoria had packed roast beef sandwiches, a thermos of gazpacho, and the ever popular peanut butter and jelly sandwiches. Morgan dispensed cold cans of soda from the ice chest. He'd asked Mrs. Duncan to join them under the shade of a huge oak tree for lunch, but she had refused, saying she had work to do indoors.

Morgan and Vic got back to work while the kids played by the side of the house.

"I'm going to have blisters soon, Morgan," Victoria complained. "Why not get some heavy machinery out here to dig this thing?"

"Would defeat my purpose. I'm trying to prove to Mrs. Duncan that all summer people aren't snobs out to use the year-rounders. That we work the same as they do."

"You picked a hard way to do it," she grumbled. She tossed more dirt on the lane, then lifted her head in alarm, looking around. "Have you seen the kids? They were over there a minute ago." She dropped her shovel and ran toward a path leading up Eagle Mountain, yelling Jake's name.

Morgan went around to the back of the house, calling their names.

"In here, Uncle Morgan." Jake poked his head out the kitchen doorway.

"I've found them, Vic," Morgan called to his sister and hastened to the back door. "What are you doing in there?"

"We're helping Grandma bake shortenin' bread," Jake explained, holding the screen door open for Morgan.

"Mrs. Duncan, I'm sorry the little scamps got away from us," Morgan apologized. He looked from one to the other of the children standing around the yellow oil cloth-covered table. Angie, flour covering the tip of her nose, was pushing a cutter into the dough. Davie was licking a spoon.

"They're no trouble, Morgan." She had a twinkle in her eye. "Reminds me of when Callie Sue was little or when her mom was a young un." A far away look came to her eyes. "My Daisy Lou loved makin' shortenin' bread and loved eatin' it more. Just like these little fellers, I reckon."

Morgan blinked, and he hoped it was the only outward sign that he'd been handed a revelation. He had assumed Mrs. Duncan was Callie's paternal grandmother because they had the same last name.

Vic knocked on the back door, and Morgan opened the screen. "Here they are," he said. "Mrs. Duncan says they're not being a bother." He turned back to Callie's grandmother. "I'm hoping Callie will help me baby-sit this evening, Mrs. Duncan. Would you mind if I used your phone?"

He excused himself to the living room and phoned Callie at

work. After she agreed to help him, he returned to the kitchen and found Vic and Mrs. Duncan sitting at the table, glasses of lemonade before them as they exchanged views on child rearing.

"Just give 'em lots of love, and they'll turn out all right," the crusty old woman advised. "As long as you add the hickory stick from time to time as needed." She chuckled.

"Now, Grandma," Vic started.

Morgan stood framed in the doorway, taking in the scene before him. He was breaking his back trying to get on Mrs. Duncan's good side, and Vic just waltzed in and started talking like they were old friends.

"I'm going back to work for a few more minutes," he said. "When you finish the cookies, we'll go. Mrs. Duncan, Callie is coming to my house after work. She said to tell you she won't be in too late."

The apprehensive look was back in the old woman's eyes and Morgan forced himself to smile and walk outside without slamming the screen door.

That old woman had let his sister and kids call her Grandma. She had taken them into her home and into her heart, if looks weren't deceiving. What had he done to deserve being treated like an outsider?

He tackled the ditch, working his annoyance off as he swung the pick and tossed dirt from the shovel. His intelligent mind sorted through the facts as he knew them, making lists just like on the yellow legal pad in his study.

Mrs. Morgan didn't like him paying attention to Callie. That much was clear. And why was that? According to Callie it wasn't a personal dislike, just a mistrust of summer people. Who was that Phillip anyway?

In midswing Morgan stopped, the pick dropping to the ground with a thud. Phillip was Callie's father! It all fit together now. The cad must have gotten Daisy pregnant during a summer fling and then left her. That's why Callie's name was Duncan. Callie had asked him indirectly how long his family had been coming to the mountains. She wanted to make sure they weren't related. That was it. It had to be.

He picked up the tools and started for the workshop. It was doubtful that any amount of shoveling would convince Mrs. Duncan he was not like Phillip, using her granddaughter for his own pleasure, then leaving her high and dry when fall came.

He was hot, tired, discouraged, and longing for a shower. He wanted to get away from this place. Here he was an outsider, and he didn't know how to belong. He was used to being in control, being respected for who he was and what he was, for his singing talent and for his shrewd business sense. Here he represented dirt under the old woman's feet.

Morgan called to Vic and the kids, loaded the ice chest and picnic basket, and sat in the van waiting for them, his eyes closed, his mind whirling with what he had figured out.

Finally his relatives trailed out of the house, Mrs. Duncan walking them out to the van. His good manners rescued him, and he thanked her for letting them picnic there.

As he drove off, the kids and Vic called their good-byes to Grandma.

"She's not your grandma," he snapped, then was aware of four pairs of startled eyes upon him.

"Sorry," he muttered and drove them home in silence.

six

Callie knocked once on the front door and immediately heard running footsteps. The door opened and Jake stood grinning up at her.

"Come on in, Callie Sue. Uncle Morgan's in the kitchen fixing dinner." He motioned her to follow him.

He had called her Callie Sue. How odd.

"Hi, Callie," Morgan greeted her. He was dressed casually in a green striped knit shirt and a pair of khaki shorts. Davie stood on a stool beside him, and Angie monopolized his other side. In one hand Morgan held a slotted spoon and in the other an apron. He tossed the apron to her. "I was hoping you'd give me a little assistance. It's Wanda's night off, and Mom and Vic left a few minutes ago."

"What are we making?" Callie asked, laying her purse on the counter and tying the apron around her waist. Lot of good a fancy apron would do her, she thought ruefully; she always spilled things on herself.

"We're making pizza," Angie answered. "You know, you're prettier than Grandma said."

"Thank you." Callie wondered if Dorothy had discussed her with the children after the surprise birthday party.

"We went to your house today," Angie said.

Callie glanced at Morgan.

"I took them with me," he explained. "They helped work on the lane."

"We sure did," Jake said. "We had a picnic, and Grandma let us make shortenin' bread. They were good."

"Grandma's a good cook," Callie replied as her mind assimilated the fact that Grandma liked the kids or she would have shooed them out of her kitchen. Besides that, she'd let them call her Grandma.

"Let's see if this pizza is as good." Morgan obviously wasn't expanding on the visit to Eagle Mountain.

Callie grated cheese, then helped clean up the kitchen while the pizza baked. They carried it to the deck and ate amid laughter and chatter. The kids were full of the different things they had seen at Grandma's and explained them to Callie as if she hadn't lived there all her life.

With supper over, the kids carried plates into the kitchen and brought back their Candy Land board game. After the third game, Morgan called a halt.

"Time to get ready for bed," he announced. "Quick baths, then to bed, little friends."

Groans and entreaties issued from the kids, but at Morgan's firm voice, they scurried to the bedroom wing of the house.

"I'll supervise Davie," Morgan told her. As soon as he headed for the bathroom, Callie rinsed the dishes for the dishwasher. She had the room spotless when Morgan returned, three kids in pajamas in tow.

"Morgan's going to tell us a story," Jake said.

Davie reached for Callie's hand and pulled her along. "Come on," he said.

Morgan tucked Jake and Davie into twin beds, then sat in the rocking chair with Angie on his lap. Callie took an upholstered chair in the corner and watched entranced as Morgan told a story of kids mountain climbing and meeting a ferocious bear. By the end of the story, the kids had tamed the bear and taken him home to live with them.

"A little corny," he said under his breath and grinned.

"It's a great story," Callie whispered back. "But they're

not asleep."

"Sing us a song, Uncle Morgan," Angie said. "The angel song."

"Then it's lights out, and you go to sleep. Promise?"

"Promise," the three kids said in unison. Callie chuckled. This obviously was the evening ritual.

"May you sleep with the angels, my little ones," Morgan crooned in his tenor voice. "May your dreams be the kind that come true. If you sleep with the angels, my little ones, little ones, then God will be smiling on you."

As he sang the verse one more time, Callie closed her eyes. The vision of Trey sprang in front of her eyes. Although she didn't know the song, the voice was the same one that sang on her stereo. She opened her eyes, and there was Morgan. Two very different personalities in one person.

He smiled at her when he finished the song, then carried Angie across the hall to her bed. Callie sat in the corner until he returned and asked Jake to say the prayer. After he kissed the boys good night, he held out his hand to Callie. Together they walked down the hall to the living room.

"Shall we sit on the deck?" Morgan asked. "Or is it too cool for you?"

"I'll be fine," she said.

Morgan grabbed an afghan from the couch and opened the french doors onto the deck. He led Callie to the platform swing and sat down beside her.

"I've been wanting to talk to you," he said as he spread the afghan around their shoulders.

"About your careers?" Callie asked. "Which one do you prefer?"

"That's the problem. I like parts of both. Callie, you know I like making records. That's the fun part of singing. I've pretty much limited myself to recording and cut out the live performances, and not just because I'm afraid. You were right years ago about the power of prayer. Each performance I asked God for strength to get through the concert and He gave it to me. I never forgot a word or a note. Now, though, I don't have the time for tours. Reporters bother me. I thought no concerts would put an end to publicity hounds, and it has to an extent. At least up here I don't have to worry about that." He reached for her hand and held it.

"What do you like about the corporation?"

"I like contributing to a company Grandad and Dad built. It's my heritage. I want it to continue as a company so Vic's kids and maybe someday my children will have the same opportunity I've had. I like the decision making. I guess I like the power."

"Is there something wrong with that? Power isn't bad. Someone has to make decisions, and I'd feel safe having you in charge of my business. You'd weigh every issue fairly and make as wise a decision as you could. Right?"

"I like to think that. But will other business leaders think I'm making wise decisions or will they think I'm an air-head singer who's been handed a corporation as a toy?"

Callie turned in the swing so she could see his face in the dim light that filtered outside from the living room lamp. Morgan shifted, too, and rearranged the afghan so that they still had cover from the cool mountain air. He pushed the swing gently with his foot.

"I suppose that depends on your decisions," Callie said thoughtfully. "You shouldn't be afraid of what others will think of your singing career. You're an individual. You can't rest on your grandad's laurels or on your father's. You have to be who you are. And you are a wonderful singer who happens to be a businessman, too."

"You think so?"

"Of course. Hey, if an actor can be President of the United States, a singer can head a large corporation. The two careers don't conflict. They could actually complement each other." Callie grinned. "You could sing at the company Christmas party."

Morgan stopped the gentle sway of the swing and sat up straight. "I've been asked to sing at Super Bowl half-time."

She raised her eyebrows at him. "What are you going to do?"

He took a deep breath and let it out slowly. "I don't want to do it. Besides the thousands at the stadium, there would be millions watching on TV—live.

"Then don't do it."

"Just like that?"

"Exactly. As a full-time singer you were busy—on the road performing and recording at home. Now that the business takes lots of your time, you've cut out the touring because it's the part you dislike and is too time consuming. Don't make an exception and go back to it. You've earned the right to do what you want."

He took her hands in his. "You have such a clear way of stating the obvious. I've gone over that very logic, then I get bogged down with—will no performances hurt my image? Will fans keep buying my records if I don't perform occasionally? I don't think so, but if not, I don't have to depend on singing for a living."

He leaned over and kissed her, not once, but twice.

"Oh," she said when he drew back.

"Yes, oh."

They stared at each other, then Callie drew back. She'd promised Grandma she wouldn't get involved with a summer person, and this wasn't how to keep that promise. But Morgan was not a typical summer person. She put her hands in her lap.

As if reading her mind, Morgan said, "I think I know who Phillip is."

Callie gasped. "You know my fa. . ." She stopped herself before she finished the sentence.

"No. I know Phillip is your father. I figured out today that Mrs. Duncan is your maternal grandmother. All along I thought she was your father's mother."

Callie stood up and walked to the deck railing. She stared out at the darkness, broken far below by lights from houses that twinkled like the stars above her. She shivered and hugged herself for warmth. The cool night air did not chill her as much as the realization that Morgan knew she didn't know who her father was.

He came up behind her and spread the afghan over her shoulders like a shawl. He pulled her back to lean on him. "Your grandmother thinks I'm like Phillip," he stated.

"Yes. She doesn't trust summer people. Especially those on Regal Mountain."

"But you trust me?"

"Yes. I've only known about Phillip for a few days. She had told me he was killed in an accident before I was born."

"And you never questioned that?"

Callie turned to face him, glad he kept his arms around her for support. "At first I did. I wanted to see pictures of him, but we didn't have any. I asked lots of questions, but Grandma never answered them, so I quit asking." She said in a small voice, "If it wasn't for you, she wouldn't have told me."

"Do you want to find your father?"

Callie was silent for a long moment, searching her heart for the truth. "I don't know. One minute I want to know who he is, to know something about his family. The next minute I never want to know a man who would turn his back on me."

Morgan nodded and pulled her closer. Callie rested her head on his chest. This was what she needed. Comfort.

"If you decide to find him, I'll help you." When she didn't respond he continued. "This has nothing to do with you. You are who you are, no matter who your parents were. You're a lovely, kind, God-fearing woman. Your ancestry has nothing to do with the kind of woman you are. Oh, your grandmother does, because she raised you and instilled her beliefs in you. But genes don't matter that much. It's what you do with them that matters."

Callie started to lean back, but he cupped her head with his hand and held it against his chest. She wanted the moment to go on and on, but it ended with the sound of the garage door opening.

"Whatever decision you make, I'll support it," he said and led her back to the swing. "But if you want to find him, we will."

Dorothy and Victoria breezed onto the deck, greeted them, and took chairs beside the swing.

"How was your night out?" Callie asked.

"More importantly," Victoria said, "how was your night in? Did the kids behave?"

"Perfect angels," Callie said.

"Now, why are they better for you than they are for me? That's kids for you. By the way, I had a pleasant visit with your grandmother today. The kids and I went to help with the lane and had a picnic. I like her. She's quite a character."

"That she is," Morgan agreed. He had nonchalantly settled his arm around Callie's shoulders and she welcomed the protective gesture. She still felt flustered from their discussion.

"Where did you go for dinner?" she asked to make conversation.

"Collett's," Victoria answered. "They have a scrumptious

cheesecake that I can't resist. Didn't you and Morgan go there? Did you try it?"

"No. I mean, we didn't try it, but we did go there."

"What do you do for entertainment, Callie?" Dorothy had wandered from the chair to the deck railing where Morgan and Callie had stood just minutes before.

"I go to movies with friends, but more often Grandma and I have friends over to visit, play music, or play dominoes."

"Do you dance at your music parties?" Victoria's animated voice held real interest. "That mountain stumble or something that we saw a few years ago. Do you remember, Morgan? We went down to Dillard for some special celebration."

"You must mean clogging," Callie said.

"Yes, that's it. Do you clog?"

"Sure. Would you like to learn how?"

Victoria chuckled. "We tried it at that festival. What a disaster. I felt like I had two left feet. Morgan wasn't any better."

"Wait a minute. I can clog circles around you, Vic," he teased. "Why don't we all go to Dillard tomorrow night? Have a little contest. Don't they have a tent show every night, Callie?"

"They do."

"I'm game. How about asking your grandmother to join us, Callie? I'll bet she's a real clogger."

"She is. I don't know if she'll come or not, but I'll ask her." Callie reluctantly stood up and smiled at Morgan. "I must be going. Tomorrow's another day at the office."

"It's nice to see you again, Callie." Dorothy led the way to the living room. "I'm looking forward to tomorrow night. And do encourage your grandmother to join us. I'd love to meet her."

"I'll ask her. Will you take the kids? I think they'd have fun."

"Only if you'll help me keep an eye on them," Vic said.

"Of course, Vic," Morgan said. "We'll each take one in tow."

Callie folded the afghan and laid it on the arm of the couch. She picked up her purse and Morgan ushered her to the door.

"I'll see you tomorrow," Callie called to the Rutherford women.

They called good night as Morgan walked her outside to her pickup.

"Remember what I said. If you want to find him, we will. If you don't, we'll never discuss it again." He pulled her close and kissed her.

When the kiss ended, Callie clung to him. "I must go," she whispered, but made no move to withdraw.

"Yes," Morgan said, but his arms tightened around her. He kissed her again and finally let her go.

"We'll pick you up around seven tomorrow night. Let's eat at the Dillard House before the clogging begins."

"Sounds good." Callie climbed into the pickup. Morgan shut the door, stepped back, and blew her a kiss, the same gesture she had seen on his TV special. Was this Trey or Morgan?

Her mind reeled as she inched her way down the mountain to stop at the gate house and insert the plastic card that opened the gate. When she had arrived earlier, Billy had stopped her and given her the card, telling her Morgan had instructed him to give it to her so she could come and go whenever she needed. She shook her head, her lips faintly curved; Morgan seemed to be after more than a friendship.

She watched the gates swing open and drove the pickup onto the highway toward home. What did he want from her and what was she willing to give? Everything, her heart answered, but her mind couldn't see a permanent relationship between them. She didn't fit into his high-powered world. She liked his family well enough, and they seemed to like her, but for all that, they were millions of dollars apart. The likelihood that he could settle down with someone like her seemed remote.

So what did he want? An affair? She didn't believe that. He was a God-fearing man. But memories of her mother and the unknown Phillip flooded her mind. For a moment she knew how her mother must have felt, loving Phillip the way she had. But did she love Morgan?

Yes, her heart answered again. She had loved Morgan for five years. For most of that time, he was a pipe dream of hers, based on what she knew of him. But the last few days had proved that in this case, fantasy and reality were the same. He was the man of her dreams, and he lived up to them. A big star, a singer, a caring man, a Christian. All those things in one man. If only he could truly love her.

Callie turned onto the dirt road from the highway and automatically slowed the pickup to a crawl, preparing herself for the bumps and ruts. They were gone! The road had been graded! She picked up speed a bit and marveled at the ride.

When the county road turned into their lane, the ruts returned, then ended again at the point Morgan and Vic had reached with their slow, painstaking labor. The light was on in the living room, and Callie parked the pickup in the shed and raced to the house.

"What happened to the road?" she demanded of Grandma as she burst into the front room.

"It was graded," Grandma replied calmly. She was sitting in the big green chair beside the lamp, one of her beloved paperback westerns in her hands.

"I know that," Callie stated. "But when, how, why? Did you hear it?"

"Whoa! Sit down and I'll tell you all about it. Want something to drink?"

"Quit stalling. That road hasn't been touched in years and now it's as smooth as velvet. What are you hiding, Grandma?"

"Nothing. Frank DeShaver came by on that big road grader of the county's and said he was ordered to come over here and get that road in shape today. He came not long after Morgan and the kids left and worked until almost dark."

"But what prompted it after so many years of neglect?" Callie stood with hands on her hips, wanting to get to the bottom of this puzzle.

"Humph," Grandma snorted. "It was politics. Frank told me it was Darrell Pressman hisself who called and told him to do it this afternoon. Seems Morgan paid him a little visit this morning and threw his weight around to get it done." Grandma didn't seem too pleased that Morgan had gone to all that trouble for them.

Callie sat down hard on the footstool in front of Grandma's chair. "Morgan did that for us?"

"Yep. He did it for you. Don't it gripe you that someone who only comes here for a few weeks a year has more say in what goes on here than us year-rounders?" She frowned.

"He may not live here year-round, but he pays a sight more money in land taxes than we do, Grandma. Even with us owning Eagle Mountain. That's undeveloped land, and it doesn't touch the kind of money Morgan and his friends pay for their big fancy homes on Regal Mountain." She got up from the footstool and stood once again with her hands on her hips, facing Grandma. "Money talks. That may not be right, but it's how the world runs. And for once we know somebody who has some power to do things. Morgan did nothing wrong. He just righted a wrong, if you want to look at it that way. He wouldn't use his influence to do anything illegal."

"No," Grandma said. "Frank said he was told to do the road, but he couldn't touch our lane since it wasn't county property. He said he's done that kind of thing before when persuaded right. But he was told Morgan was takin' care of our lane hisself."

Callie smiled a big broad smile. "See. He's a good man, Grandma. I know he's a summer person, but he's a good man. He and his family are taking me to Dillard tomorrow night for dinner and clogging. They've asked you, too. What do you say? Wouldn't you like to go? Then you'd have the opportunity to thank Morgan for all that's been done for us." She was preparing for a major battle with Grandma, but was surprised when Grandma agreed.

"Might not be a bad idea," the old woman said with a gleam in her eye. "Long as you're goin', I might as well go, too. Who all's goin' to be there?"

"Dorothy, Morgan's mother, and Victoria and the kids who you met this afternoon."

"Yep. That Vic's a good 'un. Got good kids, too." Grandma nodded her head in agreement as she got up from her chair. "Sure, I'll go." She told Callie good-night and walked toward her bedroom.

Callie heard her mutter, "Sure, I'll go. Keep my eye on things."

seven

The wind had picked up in the night and blown in a cool front that threatened rain. Morgan had awakened to fog so thick he couldn't see the great oaks that stood ten feet from his bedroom window. The fabulous view that he knew lay beyond the fog might have been only a figment of his imagination.

And what else was in his imagination? He thought Callie cared for him—but did she really? He had dreamed about her last night. When he awoke, he found himself praying that she had had a safe drive home on the curvy roads—and praying that she loved him.

Falling in love with her hadn't been love at first sight. That night five years ago in the restaurant he had been intrigued by her because she hadn't fallen all over the big star, but nothing more.

Instead, his feelings were love at second sight. On the day they had spent together filling out her college application, he had fallen for her. She had been shy at first, but then she had opened up and talked to him. More importantly, she had listened. He had felt so at ease with her, that he'd confided his hopes and fears.

Since that time, he'd unconsciously been waiting for her. He had dated other women in those years, but still had not committed himself to a lasting relationship. He had fooled himself into thinking he wasn't ready to settle down. Now he realized it was Callie who had kept him single.

He threw the light covers off and rolled out of bed, his bare feet hitting the thick carpet with a soft thud. With the habit of years, he walked to the bathroom and showered. He knew he was an anomaly in show business, but morning was his favorite time. He had grown up emulating his father, who was always dressed and ready to face the day when Morgan saw him. At a moment's notice his father could leave the house to settle a business crisis or a personal emergency. He was never caught off guard, and it was a trait Morgan admired.

Freshly shaved, clean, and dressed, Morgan headed for the kitchen and a cup of Wanda's unbeatable coffee. One of the things he looked forward to when meeting the family in the mountains was a cup of Wanda's brew and a talk with his mother, who was as early a riser as he was. He could always go to his mother's house in Atlanta, but his life was so busy there, he rarely had time for a visit. He called her regularly and they had a good relationship, but she was as busy as he was, and their good intentions to see each other rarely materialized. When they did manage to meet, they squeezed a lot into their short time together. Except this time. He had been here almost a week and had spent most of his evenings with Callie. His mornings were spent in his office, and likely as not, Dorothy was running errands, sight-seeing, or shopping in the afternoons.

He poured himself a cup and sat down at the kitchen table alone. A moment later, Dorothy walked in.

"Good morning, Morgan." Dorothy smiled at him as she crossed to the coffee maker.

"Morning, Mom." He looked at her with a straightforward gaze. "I've just been thinking about you. We haven't had time for a good visit, have we?"

Dorothy sat down across from him and smiled. "She's special, isn't she?"

"Yes, she is." He had no need to ask who. They may not have seen a lot of each other lately, but they had always communicated on the same plane.

"And does she feel the same way about you?"

"I don't exactly know." He shook his head. "I think she does, but she has a lot of ingrained biases. Her grandmother distrusts all summer people."

"You put her through college for your benefit, didn't you?" Dorothy's eyes were not accusing, just concerned.

"No," he said. "Well, not at first, but maybe it developed into that. She needed a broader background and more confidence in herself." He pushed away from the table, walked to the glass wall, and stared out at the fog. "That sounds very manipulative, as if I'm trying to change her into what I want her to be. Yet it's not that way." He stood with his back to his mother, his hands in his slacks pockets. "She's so intelligent; she needed the opportunity. It was a risk. She could have met someone at college, and I would have been out of the picture." He turned and looked at her. "But it didn't happen that way, and I'm not sure how it will turn out. I came here this summer to get to know her better, to see what might happen between us."

"You are so much like your father, Morgan. You want to have as much information as possible before you make a decision. But this time, your list of pros and cons isn't going to help." Her eyes danced as she looked at him. "Seems to me your future is in the hands of a little gal from the mountains."

He smiled wryly and acknowledged her wisdom. "You're probably right. So where do I go from here?"

"What? The dashing bachelor needs help dealing with a woman?" She laughed. "Wouldn't the tabloids have a hey-day with that!"

"It's not funny, Mother." His serious eyes asked for her understanding.

"No, it's not. But don't worry about it, Morgan. I trust

Callie's judgement—and she couldn't do better than you."

"Thanks. I hope your confidence in her and me isn't misplaced." He leaned down and kissed her cheek. Glancing at his watch, he changed the subject. "I've got to call the office and see what was accomplished with our flight attendants. I'd hate to fly to Kansas City to sit in on negotiations."

"Have you eaten?"

"No. I'll eat when Vic and the kids are up."

As if on cue, Victoria sauntered into the kitchen.

"Morning, Vic," Morgan patted her head as he passed her. "Call me when breakfast is ready."

Closeted in his study, the shrewd businessman took over, and Morgan reviewed the information he'd been faxed the previous afternoon. When Vic called him for breakfast, he told her to go ahead and eat, that he would be a few more minutes. He took another hour to complete his agenda, and he was grateful when Wanda brought in a fresh cup of coffee.

The house was empty when he finished jotting notes to himself and called his secretary again to dictate letters. A note on the refrigerator told him he was own his own for lunch. The others had gone to Asheville on an impromptu excursion with some friends and wouldn't be back until late afternoon.

Morgan called his manager and rejected the Super Bowl offer. Harry growled, but Morgan told him straight out that he wouldn't be doing any performances. He'd commit to presenting a Grammy, if asked, but not to singing in public. Callie had said he'd earned the right to do as he pleased and he agreed.

His thoughts turned to Callie. He still had to convince her grandmother that he was worthy of Callie. And there was the matter of Phillip. Callie might not know it yet, but he was certain she wouldn't be satisfied until she knew why her father had deserted her mother. Knowing the real story might make Mrs. Duncan feel better about both Phillip and Morgan. Morgan wouldn't start the search without Callie's okay, but he decided it wouldn't be long before she came to the realization that she had to know.

Left with the day to himself, Morgan prowled the house like a caged animal. The fog had turned to heavy drizzle and any thought of outside activity was nixed. He tried to read a novel, but couldn't concentrate.

His muscles cried for attention. For two days he had shoveled dirt and now they needed some exercise to ease the stiffness of the unaccustomed strain. He worked out regularly at his home gym in Atlanta or played racquetball with a friend, and he needed some sort of workout now.

Knowing it wasn't the smartest thing to do for his voice, but nevertheless determined to get outside, Morgan donned an old sweat suit and running shoes and took off into the drizzle. He ran over to the clubhouse, a fairly flat run. From there the road turned up the mountain and ran by Reynolds', past Newmans' and peaked at Houstons'. He turned around and flew down the mountain, past his own house and down, down.

He stopped when he reached Robert Garrigan's and rang the doorbell. No answer. His old pal from Atlanta was either not in or at the computer plotting his latest mystery. He didn't like being interrupted and didn't answer the door or phone when he was writing. Morgan didn't blame him. He certainly didn't allow visitors at the studio when he was recording.

He turned and started back up the mountain. After a couple of blocks, he slowed to a walk and looked over at Prescotts'. Dianne Prescott stood looking out the picture window at the rain. Although he hadn't seen her in a couple of years, in other summers in the mountains they had dated.

She had seen him and waved. He walked to the front door,

which opened before he reached the first step.

"Trey, when did you come to the mountains?" She had always called him by his stage name, probably because that was what attracted her to him, but she was as gorgeous as ever. The two years since he'd seen her hadn't aged her one day. She wore turquoise slacks and a long blousy white top trimmed in turquoise, the same color she'd been wearing the last time he'd seen her. Her eyes glittered with excitement.

"Hello, Dianne. I arrived Thursday. Yourself?"

"Just got in yesterday, in time for this dreary weather. The whole family's due in by the end of the week. Big reunion. We're having a party Saturday night. I hope you'll be able to come."

"I'll check and see," Morgan replied noncommittally.

"Come in, Trey. We can catch up on news." She looked him up and down and smiled persuasively.

"No, thanks. I'm drenched and need to finish my run before I get cold. I'll see you later, Dianne." He waved a salute and turned back for the run up the mountain, aware that Dianne stood on the porch and watched his retreat.

The last summer he'd seen her, she had just been divorced after a one year marriage. She'd wanted to continue their dating relationship and had called him in Atlanta, but he hadn't complied. He wasn't sure that as a Christian he should date her, especially since he didn't know the facts of her marriage and divorce. Besides, she was a summer date, not someone he wanted around on a permanent basis. She'd not taken his rejection well, but she seemed to have forgiven him now for ending their dating relationship.

Morgan made the rest of the jog in good time, and once inside the garage, he took off his wet shoes and socks and darted for his room. Testing his voice, he sang in the shower and heard no telltale raspiness.

He needed to write the songs for his new album. That had been one of his goals while on vacation from the corporation, if he decided to continue singing. Although he had talked only briefly with Callie about his two careers, his thoughts had solidified since last night. No concerts was an easy decision. He'd further concluded that he could put out a new album every two years without disrupting his corporate life. True, Harry would growl that he had to record one album a year, but he'd come around eventually. Harry always growled. He'd actually taken their no concerts conversation better than Morgan had thought he would.

He wanted to tell Callie. He glanced at the clock—almost twelve—he might catch her. He dressed and drove into Highridge, carefully manipulating the wet, slick turns. The receptionist at the CPA firm got wide-eyed when she saw him.

"Is Callie in?"

"She's on her lunch break," she said. "She usually brings her lunch and eats at her desk. Go on back."

"Thanks." Morgan walked down the long hallway until he reached Callie's office. She sat in her chair with her back to the door and her feet propped up on her work table, a paperback novel in her hand.

"Hi," he said softly.

She whirled in her chair, dropping the book.

"Hey, Robert's latest book," he said, picking it up and handing it back to her.

"Since you knew him, I thought I should know what he wrote. What are you doing here, Morgan?"

"I thought I'd take you to lunch."

"Oh." She smiled up at him. "That's a lovely thought, but I only have fifteen minutes left. I had an early lunch since I have a twelve forty-five appointment. Want to share?" she asked and motioned to a chair. "I have some chips left and an apple. Want a drink?" She handed him the canned soda on her desk, and he took a long drink, exulting in the fact that her lips had touched the same place as his.

I'm as silly as a teenager, he thought. Once again a teenager on a first date.

"I've decided to sing and be CEO of the Rutherford Group," he said without preamble.

She nodded. "You can do both. It just requires balance. If you see that you want to do more recording, you could appoint someone to oversee the business. However, I don't know how you'd work it if you wanted to do less singing. You can't appoint someone to take your place as a singer."

"I know. One album every two years is my plan. I've been using studio musicians for the albums since I laid off the concert tour. Most of them are the same guys who went on that last tour with me, but I just pick them up when I need them, so they aren't depending on me for a livelihood."

"Sounds like you've got it all worked out."

"Not the details and not the songs. I have a few songs that will work, but all of them aren't written. The house is empty today, so I'll be able to work this afternoon. I was hoping for a little inspiration."

"Inspiration? From me?"

He walked around the desk and pulled her to her feet and into his arms. He kissed her soundly, then stepped back.

"That ought to do it. I'm working on a love song this afternoon." He chuckled at her expression and walked to the door. "I'll see you tonight. Till then." He blew her a kiss, then walked out the door.

Notes were already flitting through his mind. By the time he arrived back on Regal Mountain, he had a full-fledged melody. He sat at the grand piano in the living room, pencil in hand, manuscript paper on the piano top, and hit keys and wrote down notes. "Callie's Song," he said and hummed before he played a few more notes and scribbled them down. Within an hour, he had the entire melody down, including chords.

If he could get the others done that quickly, he could meet with the arranger in a couple of weeks and get each score finished. Normally he used a violin, drums, and a bass guitar, but on occasion, he'd add a sax and other brass instruments. Each song demanded different instruments to make the emotion come through.

"We're home," Vic called from the kitchen.

Morgan had been so absorbed in his work, he hadn't heard the car pull in. The chatter of kids coming inside and the ringing of the phone coincided.

"I'll get it," Vic said.

"Come listen to this," Morgan called to the others. The kids and Dorothy joined him in the living room. He played the new song.

"It's beautiful," Dorothy said. "What's it called?"

"I don't have all the words down yet," he hedged. She looked over his shoulder at the title he had written down and raised her eyebrows.

"Mmm. She'll love it," she said.

"Morgan, a message for you," Vic said as she waltzed into the living room.

Morgan's mind flew to the labor negotiations. "Charlie?"

"No, dear brother. A voice out of your past."

He immediately knew. "Dianne?"

"Yes. She invited us to a party Saturday night. I asked if we could bring a guest and of course she agreed, not knowing I meant Callie."

Morgan frowned. "That should prove interesting. I told

Callie we'd pick her and Mrs. Duncan up tonight at seven.
So everybody be ready by a quarter to. I'd better call the
office again." He took his music notebook and headed back
to his study. He wanted to write the poem that would make
this especially Callie's song, but he needed peace and solitude to do that.

Not to make a liar out of himself, he called the office and
learned the flight attendants' negotiations were hitting some
snags. He called Kansas City and talked to Charlie Lockard,
who had flown out there the day before. By the time he'd
finished tying up details, it was time to get ready for clogging
at Dillard. "Callie's Song" would have to wait.

At fifteen minutes before seven, the family climbed into
the van and set off for the Duncans'. Vic commented on the
newly-graded road, but Morgan didn't explain his part in it.
As he turned the van onto the rutted lane, he noticed a red
Trans-Am parked in front of the house. Callie, Mrs. Duncan,
and a strange man sat in the rocking chairs on the front porch.

Morgan left the others in the van and walked to the porch,
assessing the man on his way. Although he was sitting, Morgan could tell he was lean and fairly tall, but not as tall as
himself. He had straight blond hair and sported a thick mus-
tache. He was laughing with the women, but kept his gaze on
Morgan.

"Good evening, Morgan." Callie stood as he climbed the
slab rock steps. "I'd like you to meet Joe Lowery. Joe, this is
Morgan Rutherford."

The two men shook hands, much like two boxers eyeing
one another in the ring, assessing the other's ability and chance
at success.

"Joe had business in Highridge and stopped off here hoping he could eat supper with us," Mrs. Duncan announced,
her eyes dancing. "He does that whenever he's in town. He's

a banker in Franklin," she informed Morgan proudly.

"I see," Morgan said. After a pregnant pause, he added, "Why don't you join us for the evening, Joe. We're going to Dillard for dinner."

"Thanks, Morgan, I'd like that. I haven't visited with Callie Sue and Grandma in quite a while, and I was looking forward to it." Joe accepted the invitation with a big grin. Somehow Morgan had known he would.

"Tell you what," Joe continued. "Why don't I drive Callie Sue and Grandma down there since it's a straight shot from Dillard to Franklin for me to go on home. Then you can bring these two ladies back here later."

The evening was not going at all like Morgan had planned, but he smiled and agreed to Joe's plan, since Grandma looked at him as if he had no choice.

Morgan ended up following Joe's car down the steep and curvy road to Dillard and parking next to him on the huge parking lot beside the Dillard House.

The country meal was served family style with large bowls of corn-on-the-cob, green beans, mashed potatoes, gravy, ham, fried chicken, and biscuits. Conversation halted as bowls were passed around. The kids provided a continuous chatter from then on, and the adults chimed in, soon breaking off into their own conversational groups.

Morgan watched the various participants. Mrs. Duncan eyed Dorothy suspiciously for a short while, then seemed to warm to her as Vic played moderator. Callie conversed at length with Joe, but tried to involve Morgan, too. He didn't know the people they discussed, and although Callie explained a bit, the conversation meant nothing to him. To add injury to insult, Joe asked him what he did for a living. Normally Morgan would enjoy not being recognized as Trey, but this meant that Callie hadn't talked about him to Joe. Morgan would have thought his name would have come up. He found himself talking to the kids and letting the adult conversation flow around him. He didn't like it, not one little bit.

Clogging in the tent show was as little fun for him as the dinner party had been, even though the main guitarist, a man at least in his sixties, knew his music and conveyed it to the audience. A young woman in a short, square dance dress and shiny white patent leather shoes with taps illustrated the mountain dance. When the audience was asked to join them on stage, all the kids, Vic, and Joe trooped forward. Morgan, however, wasn't in the mood to join the group.

At last Callie persuaded him to follow her. Try as he might, though, the steps were too difficult for him, requiring that he move from the knee down, holding the upper body straight. At the partner switch, Callie clogged with Joe, and Morgan and Vicki sat down. The next partner switch, Callie clogged with little Davie, and Joe claimed a seat beside Morgan.

"How long have you been here?" Joe asked suddenly.

"Almost a week," Morgan answered. "Why?"

Joe grinned his lazy grin. "Just wondering how long you'd been seeing Callie Sue."

"Almost a week," Morgan repeated.

"Didn't lose any time," Joe observed. His eyes held a glint of amusement. "I appreciate you sharing her tonight. I've not been able to see her in quite awhile." His eyes turned thoughtful as he continued. "I may be out of line here, since I just met you, but don't hurt her."

"I have no intention of hurting her," Morgan protested.

"Just see that you don't. She's an awfully special person, and she feels indebted to you."

Morgan digested this information. "I thought you didn't know who I was?"

"Just wanted to see how you'd take not being recognized.

Back to Callie. She's grateful to you for educating her, and she's built you up into some kind of hero."

The dance was over, and Joe and Morgan stood as Callie and David walked back to them. Joe's revelation had been a blow. Morgan knew Callie was grateful, she'd told him several times, but he didn't want that to be the basis for their relationship. He hadn't mentioned that check to her again, and now he decided to cash it. If she started paying him back, maybe she'd lose that grateful attitude.

After goodbyes to Joe, the rest loaded into the van for the ten-mile drive back home. The kids were quiet, tired from a late night. The women spoke softly among themselves, leaving Morgan alone to brood.

"Morgan?" Callie's voice interrupted his thoughts. She was sitting in the captain's chair across from the driver's seat and leaned toward him so they could have a private conversation.

"Yes, Callie?"

"Thank you for inviting Joe. I'm sorry I didn't get to talk with you. Joe and I are old friends, and I haven't seen him in quite some time," she explained.

"You're welcome." He knew he was being short with her, but he couldn't seem to help himself. He was jealous. For the first time in his life, he was jealous. Not that his other women friends hadn't had flirtations when he was around. They had. But he'd known all he had to do was give them a sign he wanted them beside him, and instantly they'd be there. With Callie, he didn't think that would work. He knew she cared for him—but when an old friend came calling, she showed that she truly cared for him, too. Morgan, however, wanted her all to himself.

As they turned onto the dirt road, Callie again attempted conversation. "I didn't mention it at lunch, but we are grateful for your influence in getting the road graded for us."

"You're welcome," Morgan muttered. There was that word

again, grateful.

"Grandma is impressed with your persistence in getting our lane smooth, too," she added.

Terrific, thought Morgan. What is that supposed to mean? That I should get over here tomorrow and get the job finished? He immediately dismissed that. Callie was too straightforward to manipulate him that way.

He knew he was acting like a spoiled child—but he had hoped that the two of them could have laughed together tonight, conversing with his mother and Callie's grandmother. As it was, he'd have to ask Vic how the two older women had gotten along.

He brought the van to a halt and hopped out to walk around and open the side door for Grandma, and then Callie's door. He walked them to the porch. The porch light shone brightly, and flying insects of various sizes and shapes buzzed around it.

Grandma held out her hand to Morgan. "Thanks for takin' us tonight, Morgan." With a mischievous light in her eyes, she added, "And I'm glad you asked Joe." She stepped inside the door, but Morgan could still hear her soft chuckle.

Morgan took Callie's hands in both of his and pulled her around the corner of the house where shadows gave some privacy. The good-night kiss didn't last long. After all, his family was sitting in the van, and there was no telling where Mrs. Duncan was.

"Callie, see me tomorrow night?"

"Yes," she whispered.

"I'll be here after work, and we'll decide what we want to do."

"Okay." He gave her another kiss. "Good night, Morgan," Callie said softly and stepped inside.

Morgan strode to the van with a much lighter step.

eight

Callie waited until she heard the van roar into life and start out the drive before she turned off the porch light. She stood in the dark a moment longer, then sighed and turned on the lamp in the living room. Grandma ambled in from her bedroom.

"What did you think of the evening?" Callie asked.

"Well, it was nice of him to ask Joe."

"Yes," Callie said. "He was a good sport about it. He's going to pick me up here tomorrow evening after work." She walked over to the fireplace and looked at the picture of her mother on the mantle. When Grandma's opinion wasn't forthcoming, she spun around. "Aren't you going to say summer people and year-rounders don't mix?"

"No. You know that. Money makes a big difference in a person's life. Makes them expect different things. But I reckon Morgan's a good man. He can't help being born rich, and his ma's real proud of him. And a ma can generally tell how good their young uns turn out. That Vic's a good un, too."

"Morgan's a gentleman."

"Oh, he may be a gentleman, but he's also a full growed man, and he's a man who gits what he wants. Don't think I've been fooled by his manners and his hard work on our lane. He's after you, and he intends to get you. He's just biding his time, tryin' to get on my good side." Grandma gave a sly smile.

"And is he on your good side?"

"Hmm," Grandma said noncommittally. "I know he's

already got you on his side. But be careful, Callie Sue. Don't give in to him."

"Grandma!" Callie exclaimed.

"Let's call a spade a spade, Callie Sue. I didn't marry Orie because he was the only man around. I married him because I loved him and wanted to live with him and bear his children. I know how it is. I've been there. And so has Dorothy. Don't think she don't know what's goin' on. She told me she'd never seen him so determinedly pursue anyone before. Them's her words, 'determinedly pursue.'"

Callie stretched her arms over her head and yawned. She didn't want to continue this conversation. Grandma looked like she was warming up to a lecture. Callie claimed tiredness and the need to get up early in the morning for work, and then she fled to her room to be alone with her thoughts.

So Morgan was determinedly pursuing her. Good. Because she knew she had fallen deeply in love with him, and she needed some assurance that he might feel the same way.

She was still amazed that a super star like Trey could be such a fine man. A Christian, too. His family upbringing had stayed with him even though he must have been tempted by the trappings of show business. Not that she knew much about show business, but she read the tabloid headlines while she waited in supermarket lines.

The first time she saw his picture on the cover, she had almost fainted. That had been the summer before her college days. With the innocence of a teenager, she had asked Morgan about it the next time they met to discuss her financial matters. He had discounted as pure fiction his alleged liaison with an actress. The picture had been taken at the Grammy Awards months earlier. He had been standing beside the actress, but she wasn't his date. Since then he had been on the cover each time a new album came out. Publicity, he told her. He wasn't having an affair, he hadn't been abducted by aliens, and he wasn't running away to join a guru in India. He assured her he was a dedicated Christian and his morals were high. Certainly he was a gentleman.

He had behaved well tonight, although she could see the thunderclouds on his forehead. She thought he might even be jealous. Not that jealousy was a good emotion to arouse in someone, but it did mean he wanted her to himself.

Joe had sure played up to her. If she didn't know better, she'd have thought he was interested in her, instead of feeling brotherly toward her the way he always had. He knew how she felt about Morgan; they had discussed it on their trips back and forth to school. When he had told her goodbye tonight, he had confided that he'd wanted to see what kind of man Morgan was. He'd liked him, he said, though he hadn't expected he would.

❧

The next day, Callie slipped an extra piece of peach pie in her lunch sack, hoping Morgan would join her during the noon hour. She was disappointed when her lunch hour came and went without Morgan appearing at her office door.

The minutes between four and five dragged by as Callie consulted her watch every five minutes. At exactly five, she hopped in the pickup and swung it onto the highway.

She was unprepared for the sight that met her eyes when she turned into her lane. Morgan and another man were resting on their shovels. As she drew nearer, she recognized Robert Garrigan from the cover picture of the mystery she was reading. Both men were dressed in cut-off shorts and tee-shirts, both were covered with dirt and sweat, and both sported wide triumphant grins as she pulled the pickup to a stop.

"We're finished. What do you think?" Morgan gestured down the wide sweep of lane. A drainage ditch on each side framed the smooth surface between.

"Looks wonderful. But I'll give it the ultimate driving test. Hop in."

The men jumped in the back of the pickup, hauling the pick and shovels after them. Morgan gave the go ahead sign to Callie, and she drove slowly up the lane, then increased her speed.

"I can't thank you enough," Callie told Robert after Morgan introduced them. She shook his hand and extended her hand to Morgan. He took it, only to pull her into his arms.

"You can do better than that," he said, stealing a quick kiss.

"What? You expect favors for work?" Callie teased.

"Any way I can get them," Morgan leered.

The glow of accomplishment was on both men's faces. Callie demanded an explanation.

"After I finished my office work early this morning, I called Rob and asked him if he was up for the experience of a lifetime. He accepted and we came right over. I didn't anticipate working all day, but we had accomplished enough by lunchtime, we thought we'd just keep at it. Grandma fed us lunch."

"And what a lunch," Robert chimed in. "Real home cooking."

"Then we got back on the lane, only taking time out for some water breaks. Speaking of which, I could use some right now."

"Yes, and not just on the inside," Callie said and laughed. "You're filthy. Come on, rest on the porch, and I'll bring out something cold."

She ran into the house and found Grandma lifting a tray of iced tea. "I heard you drive in, so I figured they'd be quittin'."

"They're finished."

Grandma smiled. "Two able-bodied men can do a lot more

physical labor than the two of us."

Callie took the tray from her and carried it to the porch.

"Get your swimsuit, Callie," Morgan said. "We'll have a swim, then have dinner. Sound okay?"

"Great." She left the two men laughing on the front porch while she stuffed her suit, cover-up, a towel, and some makeup into a canvas shopping bag.

"Ready?" she asked, back on the porch in record time. Morgan and Robert got to their feet, and Morgan took her bag, then tossed it in the air and caught it.

Callie laughed. Morgan P. Rutherford III, alias Trey, was playing like a schoolboy. Quite out of character for him—but then digging a ditch was a bit out of character, too. What would his corporate officers say if they saw him now? And what would his fans say if they saw this side of the singer?

"Let's go." Morgan took her hand and pulled her toward the van. "Don't worry, Grandma, I won't keep her out too late," he called.

Robert was shaking Grandma's hand and telling her he'd enjoyed lunch, and Callie could tell Grandma liked him. Morgan helped her into the van and yelled for Robert to cut the chatter so they could get to the pool.

"Grandma?" Callie echoed Morgan's word, her brows raised.

"She said Mrs. Duncan was too high and mighty, so I might as well call her Grandma like everybody else." He grinned triumphantly.

Callie nodded.

"We've made great strides today, Callie."

"You must have. I know she's impressed that you worked on the lane yourself instead of using money to hire someone else to do the hard work."

"I would have, but I knew her low opinion of summer people,

so I had to show her a different side. Come on, Rob," he yelled out the window.

As soon as Robert was in, Morgan took off, the van humming along the lane.

"Smooth as silk," Morgan bragged.

"Smooth as velvet," Robert added.

"Smooth as butter," Callie chimed in.

They described the road in as many ways as they could until they arrived at Regal Mountain. Morgan dropped Robert off at his house and urged the van up the steep climb to his own home.

He helped Callie out of the van and draped an arm around her shoulder as he ushered her into the house. "We'll change here and walk to the pool."

"Hi, Callie, Morgan," Dorothy greeted them as they swung through the living room on their way to change. "Morgan, what have you been up to? You're covered with dirt."

"Rob and I finished Callie's road. It's as smooth as glass," he said with a wink at Callie. "I feel as if I've just finished a corporate merger or had a record go platinum. And we're going to celebrate. I'll meet you back here, Callie."

She changed quickly into her suit and a white terry-cloth cover-up. The living room was empty when she returned. She wandered onto the deck and gloried in the fantastic view. Was it just a week ago tomorrow that Morgan had brought her here for that birthday party? She'd seen him so much since then, that she felt she knew him well. Well enough to turn a schoolgirl crush into full-fledged love, the deep love a woman has for a man. If only she knew for sure how he felt about her.

"Ready?"

She turned at Morgan's voice. His hair was wet. Obviously he'd thought it better to get some of the dirt off before polluting the pool.

Holding hands, they walked to the pool, a distance of about three blocks. Only one other house separated Morgan's house from the clubhouse.

The fenced-in, blue, kidney-shaped pool was three times the size of the average back yard variety. A handful of young people were grouped on one side of the pool, music blasting from their portable radio. As they approached the pool, Robert pulled up in his low slung sports car.

"Perfect timing," he called as he climbed out of the car. They claimed the corner spot, the furthest away from the noisy young people, and set up camp, towels laid down in a row. The teens had recognized Morgan and were watching him with fascination.

"I'm headed in," Morgan announced. "Coming, Callie?"

"In a minute." She watched Morgan mount the diving board. He executed a perfect jackknife that barely splashed water and came up gasping for air.

"Is it that cold?" Callie called. It was only June, and the cool mountain night air would keep the water from warming.

"No, just takes getting used to. Take the plunge. It's better to do it all at one time." Morgan began swimming curvy laps.

"Are you going in, Robert?"

"Sure. I've worked up a good sweat today."

"Yes, I know how hard you worked. Thanks again. Fixing that lane would have taken Grandma and me several months of Saturday afternoons." She paused as one of Morgan's songs came on the radio. She glanced at him, but he showed no reaction to hearing his own voice, his smooth strokes still steady and rhythmic. Callie turned back to Robert. "How did you let Morgan talk you into manual labor? It's not what I associate with a mystery writer."

"I'm always looking for new experiences. Material for my stories, you know. Just might put this experience in my next book. Morgan told me about Grandma too, and I wanted to meet her. He said she was one character I should write about. Besides, I got to spend the day talking with Morgan, and it's been a long time since we've spent that much time together. He's a special guy."

"Yes, he is," Callie agreed.

A car droned in the distance, then grew louder, until a white convertible pulled into the parking area. Robert and Callie both turned to watch a tall brunette alight gracefully from the car. Robert's eyebrows arched skyward.

"Dianne Prescott," he muttered. "Here comes trouble with a capital T."

"Oh?"

Dianne sauntered through the gate and waved prettily to Robert and Callie as she headed for the group of teens.

"Ten-minute warning. We have early dinner reservations." She glanced at the pool. "Trey," she purred.

"Hello, Dianne."

"Hi, yourself. Did you get my message? I talked to Victoria about the party. Can you come?" The radio had been turned off as the young people gathered their belongings, and her voice easily carried to Callie and Robert on their towels.

"I'm still not sure. I'll let you know before Saturday."

He swam to the edge of the pool toward his towel. Dianne walked around and stood beside him as he heaved himself out of the water.

"Hey, I thought you two were coming in?" he called.

"We are," Callie answered. She didn't know why, but she wanted to be by him, some primitive urge to stake her territory, she supposed. She slipped off her cover-up.

"Aren't you going to introduce me to your friend, Robert?" Dianne cooed.

"Sure. Callie, this is Dianne Prescott. Or is it Newcomb?"

"Prescott. I took my maiden name back after my divorce. That was a mistake, but past history now and best forgotten." She waved her hand airily. "I'm glad I've run into you, Robert. We're having a party Saturday night. Our house. Eight o'clock. You may bring a date." She cast a glance at Callie.

"Thanks, Dianne. What's the occasion?"

"Family reunion. First time in many years we'll all be in the mountains at once. The whole family will be here for a month. That crew over there," she nodded toward the teens, "are my nieces and nephews. Jerry's, P.J.'s, and Sandra's kids. This is the first time P.J.'s had his kids since his divorce."

"I haven't seen your family in ages. Might be fun," Robert said.

Morgan watched the interaction and reached his arm toward Callie. She did nothing to resist when he pulled her down beside him and pushed her unceremoniously into the water, before he jumped back in beside her.

She came up gasping for air. "Not cold? It's broken ice!" she exclaimed.

"Race you to the board and back," he challenged.

She didn't answer, but started for it, knowing that even with her head start, she couldn't beat him. She had watched his even strokes and figured he must have a pool in Atlanta.

He beat her easily and stood waiting for her at the shallow end of the pool. Callie conceded defeat and dove under the water to grab both his feet. He went under. In a lightning quick move, he changed directions and retaliated from behind, lifting her by her waist and tossing her into the water as if she were a featherweight.

Callie came up sputtering. "I think we're even."

"Probably." He was a foot away, treading water. "If you do any other despicable thing, I can't even answer for what might happen to you."

Callie glanced across the water at Dianne and Robert. Even from this distance, she could see the icy set to Dianne's face and the fascinated stares of the teens. Robert was grinning.

"Coming in, Robert?" Callie coaxed. "The water's great!"

"Sure it is," he drawled. "I heard your reaction. Broken ice."

With backward glances at Trey, Dianne's youth group trooped out the gate and Dianne followed them. "I'll see you Saturday night," she called over one shoulder.

No one replied for a moment, until Robert tossed off a nonchalant, "Sure thing."

"Do you know Trey?" Callie heard one of the girls ask her aunt.

"Very well," Dianne answered.

Callie swam to the ladder and climbed out, running for her towel to warm up. Morgan followed at a more leisurely pace.

"I don't believe Dianne likes you," Robert said dryly to Callie, "even though she thinks we're a couple." He grinned.

"Hands off, buddy," Morgan said. "She's mine. I saw her first."

"Just my luck," Robert moaned. "How'd you meet this fellow, Callie?"

Callie glanced at Morgan for approval, and he gave a barely perceptible shrug of his shoulders. "Morgan put me through college. He gave me a scholarship. I don't know where I'd be if it weren't for him."

Morgan straightened. He didn't like that grateful note in her voice.

Robert looked hard from one to the other. "I smell a story."

Callie shivered as a breeze blew across her damp skin.

"Cold?" Morgan murmured.

"I'm okay," she answered.

"Am I glad I didn't go in," Robert said. "Although I could

use a shower and a good meal. Where are you taking us, Morgan?" He laughed at his friend's expression. "You did say we were celebrating, didn't you?"

Morgan scowled good-naturedly as Robert included himself in the dinner invitation. "Think you can round up a fourth? I'm not sharing Callie anymore."

"Think I should ask Dianne?"

"Not on your life." Callie could sense the seriousness in Morgan's tone and wondered what his relationship was with Dianne. She wanted to ask, but refrained. Maybe he would volunteer some information.

"Just teasing. I'll call Marilyn. She arrived yesterday to visit her parents." Robert picked up his towel. "Want a ride?"

"No, we'll walk," Morgan said. "I need some time alone with Callie."

"So, where are we going? Black tie or Bermuda shorts?" Robert leaned against the open door of his car.

"Men! Always concerned with what they're going to wear," Callie teased. "I'm wearing what you saw me in earlier."

"Of course," Robert said. "How about Murphy's? I could meet you there."

"Good idea," Morgan agreed. "Eight-thirty? I'll call for reservations. If it doesn't work out, I'll ring you."

Robert nodded and climbed into his car. With a quick wave, he backed around and headed down the mountain.

Arm in arm, Callie and Morgan walked toward his house. "I forget how petite you are until I'm right beside you," he said.

"I never forget how tall you are," Callie returned. "I like Robert. He seems like a good friend."

"He's my best friend. I haven't seen much of him lately, but I enjoyed our visit today."

"He said the same thing."

"Sometimes I get too involved in work and don't take enough

time to be with the people I care about."

"Is that why you've taken some time off this summer? How long do you plan to stay?" She tried to sound as nonchalant as she could, but she had to know.

He smiled down at her. "I'll be here another week, then I'll come back on weekends. I've been working in the mornings, calling the office to stay on top of things. Looks as if I'm not as indispensable as I thought."

"Does it bother you that things are going well without you? That could give you more time for your songs."

"That's what I've been thinking, too. I've finished one and have the lyrics for another. Usually I do the melody first, but not always." He squeezed her shoulder. "Enough about business, I'm on vacation. Let's talk about other things, like why didn't you try some other tactic in the pool? Something that would have justified me doing something like this?" He stopped walking and took her in his arms, slowly lowering his lips to hers. She clung to him like a sailor to a life raft tossed in a storm. He pulled her closer, but the beep of a horn brought her back to the reality that they were kissing at the side of the road. They broke apart.

Victoria and the kids sailed by with Jake leaning out the window with a whistle. The other kids waved and grinned as if they had caught Uncle Morgan doing something wrong.

"Aren't nieces and nephews wonderful?" Morgan asked.

"I don't know." A thought struck her. She might actually have half-brothers and half-sisters. Maybe even nieces and nephews. She turned startled eyes to Morgan, who looked as if he were reading her thoughts. A concerned line creased his brow.

"Have you decided? Do you want to find him?"

"Yes," she said immediately. "No," she amended. "I don't know."

nine

"Let's go change," Morgan suggested. "Then we'll talk about it." He took Callie's hand as they walked the remaining few yards to his house.

Inside, Vicki's kids had destroyed the quiet of the house. They ran around laughing and giggling. "K-I-S-S-I-N-G," Josh sang out when Morgan and Callie entered the living room.

Morgan winked at Callie. "You can go ahead and rinse the chlorine off. I'll call Murphy's and then clean up."

With kids all around, Morgan didn't bring up the subject of Callie's father again until they were on their way to Highridge. "So," he slid into the topic, "you don't know if you want to find him or not."

Callie took a deep breath and let it out. "I want to know who he was if it turns out he cared about my mother and there was some reason he never returned to her. But what if he left on purpose? What if he didn't want the responsibility of a child?"

"That's the risk you'd have to take. The truth may not be what you want to hear. But will you be satisfied with a question mark for your father?"

Callie closed her eyes. "This is hard, Morgan. I've prayed about it, but I still don't have an answer. I don't want to hurt Grandma, and I don't want to be hurt myself. I keep thinking that it makes no difference. It doesn't change who I am. But there are so many unanswered questions. What if I have half-brothers and half-sisters? What if I've inherited some strange disease?"

"Don't borrow trouble, Callie. But if we find him, you must be prepared for the worst. He may not want to meet you or—"

"I may not want to meet him," Callie interrupted. "I just want to know the story."

"Then we'll find him," Morgan said with finality.

"Where do we start?"

"I'm not sure. Let me talk to some people. It can't be that hard to find someone who lived on Regal Mountain twenty-four years ago."

"What if he didn't live on the mountain? He could have been visiting. Grandma saw him once in town. Maybe he lived there for the summer."

Morgan nodded. "That's possible." He turned his sports car into Murphy's parking lot. "I don't see Robert's car," he commented. "They must not be here yet."

"Tell me about Marilyn," Callie prompted as he helped her out of the car.

"Marilyn's a good person. You'll like her. I've known her about six years. Her dad owns the Byer Drug chain. Instead of working for him, she struck out on her own and is quite a successful stockbroker in New York."

"Does she see Robert often?"

"I don't know. I met her here when she was visiting her parents. I think that's where Robert met her, too. They've been friends for quite some time. I know he sees her whenever he's in New York at his publisher's, but I don't think there's anything romantic between them." He shook his head, a brief movement. Callie had noticed earlier that all his movements and gestures were abbreviated, as if the slightest signal from him was to be obeyed. She'd seen Trey do that same motion on his TV special as he communicated with his band.

"There he is," he said and lifted a hand toward his friend. Morgan and Callie stood by the door to Murphy's and waited for Robert to park his car and join them.

"Marilyn will be a little late," Robert said in greeting. "She said by the time we finish hors d'oeuvres she'll be here."

The restaurant bustled with people, but they were seated immediately at a table near the fireplace. Booths lined each wall, while round tables dotted the floor.

Across the room, Morgan spotted Dianne Prescott with her family. Adults sat around one large table, while the younger members of the Prescott clan sat at a table beside them. One of her brothers was taking candid snapshots of the group.

Callie looked to see what had captured Morgan's interest.

"A friend of yours?" she asked, then regretted her words the minute they slipped out. His relationship with Dianne was none of her business.

"I dated her several years ago," Morgan said. "There was nothing between us. Just friendship."

Several heads had turned toward them, including Dianne's.

"Hi, Trey," she said and waved.

Morgan raised his hand and smiled. "I think we may be descended upon." A moment later, three of the Prescott teenage girls edged up to the booth and asked for Trey's autograph. Without hesitation, he scribbled his pseudonym on a menu, a cloth napkin, and a note pad. Dianne's brother snapped a picture as Morgan teased them. After gushing about his great albums, the girls left amid many giggles.

"There'll be a few more, then we'll be left alone," Morgan told her. "Once it starts, it goes on for awhile."

Sure enough, another group of teens approached, followed by another. Within minutes, the furor died down. Callie figured every teen in the place now owned a genuine Trey autograph.

By the time they finished their shrimp cocktail, an older gentleman, who'd been sitting with the Prescott's earlier, stopped by their table.

Morgan stood and shook his hand. "Cooper Prescott, it's been too long. How are things with you?"

"Fine, fine," he replied. "Real fine now that I have all my family around me for the summer. I was sorry to hear about your father, Trey. We were out of the country when he died. Please accept our sympathy."

"Thank you," Morgan replied.

"You are coming to our party Saturday night, aren't you?"

"We hope to," Morgan said.

"Good, good. We'll visit then." Mr. Prescott returned to his seat.

"Callie, would you like to go to the Prescotts' party Saturday night? Are you going, Rob?"

"I hadn't asked Marilyn yet, but I'm game."

"Callie? Vic's going, too."

"Yes, that would be nice," she said. But from the looks she'd received from Dianne, she wondered what she'd gotten herself into. She'd never felt very secure the few times she'd been around summer people when they'd come into the office. Going to a summer folk party might not be a good idea. She tried to ignore the table to their right, but she was aware of piercing stares from several members of the Prescott family.

Morgan was also aware of the daggers Callie was receiving from Dianne, and, in fact, from several of the Prescott group. Mrs. Prescott kept glancing their way. Surely she wasn't upset that he was out with someone other than her daughter. What did she expect? He had not been out with Dianne for over two years now. And her brother was a puzzle, too. He had more than once caught Jerry—or was it P.J.?—casting a curious glance at Callie. He had never kept the two older brothers straight. They were so much older than Dianne and Sandra that they had no longer been part of the Prescott household when he was on the scene.

Maybe taking Callie to their party was a mistake. And yet he wanted to go. Some perverseness in his nature wanted him to flaunt Callie to all his friends. And he knew the whole mountain would be there.

The Prescotts were a close group, but they threw a wonderful party, he remembered from summers past. He genuinely liked them, yet he was relieved when they left.

A moment later, Marilyn arrived. Morgan stood and kissed her on the cheek. Robert introduced the two women, and Marilyn extended her hand. Callie liked her instantly. The dark-haired beauty was open and friendly, her brown eyes dancing from Morgan to Callie as if she were assessing something. Callie heard her say softly, "You were right, Robert." She didn't explain her remark, but exchanged a conspiratorial look with her friend.

The waiter came and took their orders, and the foursome settled down to some lighthearted conversation. Marilyn was an entertaining woman, telling of her adventures in New York with her firm. She and Robert exchanged several secretive glances that led Callie to believe that something was between them besides just friendship.

After their meal, Marilyn and Callie excused themselves and threaded their way through the tables toward the ladies' room.

"I'm glad Morgan's found you," Marilyn said without preamble as soon as the two women were alone.

Callie didn't know what to say. "Found me?"

"Yes. You do love him, don't you? Robert said you did, and it looks that way to me."

Callie stared into her new friend's eyes. "Yes, I do," she admitted with a sigh.

"No reason for sighs. It's just as obvious that he loves you. He needs to settle down, and you're just the one he's been looking for."

"Thank you," Callie said and laughed, liking this woman more and more. "And what about you and Robert?"

"Tit for tat, huh?" Marilyn asked. "All right. We've been friends for a long time."

"Not good enough," Callie teased. "I was honest with you."

"Can you keep a secret?"

Callie nodded.

"I arranged this trip to the mountains when I knew Robert would be home. We've been seeing quite a bit of each other lately when he comes to New York." Callie heard an unsure quality in Marilyn's voice that belied her sophistication.

"Does he know how you feel?" Callie asked.

"Not in so many words. But I show it, don't I?"

"To me, yes. To Morgan, no. He says you're just friends. Sometimes men have to be hit on the head before they realize what's going on."

"You may be right," Marilyn agreed. "Shall we join our thickheaded men?"

Morgan looked up as Callie and Marilyn made their way back to the table. He rose to his feet beside Robert and pulled out Callie's chair, then sat back down.

"Robert, when did you start writing mysteries?" Callie asked. "You're very young to have published so many."

Morgan noted that Callie leaned across the table toward Robert as she spoke. He liked that about her. She focused on whoever she was talking to, making that person feel special.

"Such a flatterer, Callie. I've been writing since I was twelve, but nothing got published until I was twenty-seven. Since then I've been turning out two mysteries a year."

"Two a year! How can you think of that many plots?"

Robert shrugged. "They just come when I need them. I have one detective, Sinclair, who's in every book, and in a way there's a definite pattern to a mystery. I fill in the outline. The hardest part for me is finding the right names. Maybe I'll use Callie next time I need a lady in distress. Or better yet, a villainess," he teased.

Callie laughed. "Have you used Marilyn in a book yet?"

"She's Sinclair's girlfriend. Sometimes she's not in a book, but usually she puts in an appearance. Lately she's gotten involved in the plots."

"Isn't that interesting?" Callie smiled a mischievous smile at Morgan. He watched the glint in her eyes and suddenly knew that Robert and Marilyn were more than just friends. He wondered if Rob knew.

He looked at his friend and could almost see the lightning that snapped between him and Marilyn.

"Marilyn, are you ready to go?" Robert asked in a dazed voice. "I think we'll be off."

"Sounds good to me," Morgan agreed. He left money for the check. Robert and Marilyn walked ahead, holding hands. Morgan took Callie's hand and followed.

In the parking lot they said good night, promising to see each other at the Prescotts' party Saturday night.

As Morgan and Callie headed along the curvy road to Callie's, she laughed out loud. "Was it my imagination or did Robert just realize he's in love with Marilyn?"

"I thought so, too," Morgan agreed. "But you knew, didn't you?"

"I suspected."

"Robert's a wonderful guy, but he's a writer. He gets preoccupied sometimes and doesn't see the tree for the forest. He's a master at describing characters' emotions, so I'm a bit surprised he didn't recognize his own. Of course, I didn't see

it, either," he admitted. "But I'm perfectly aware of my own."
One glance at her face and he realized this wasn't the time
for a declaration of love. "I'm having a great vacation," he
said instead. "And you're the reason."

ten

What was wrong with her? With her elbows propped on the high bureau, Callie rested her chin in her hands and stared at her reflection in the old mirror. She was certain Morgan had been going to tell her he loved her, just as she had prayed and dreamed for years. Yet, she knew she'd turned beseeching eyes to him, begging him not to say those three words.

Why? Was it her promise to Grandma that she wouldn't get involved with a summer person? She didn't think so. Even Grandma liked Morgan now.

"You are an idiot," she told her reflection in a low voice that wouldn't wake up Grandma. "But we're worlds apart. It isn't that silly summer person thing. It's the difference in the have and have-not society. He has so much. Yet," she argued with her reflection, "he hasn't abused his wealth."

She remembered one of their topics at dinner. Her dinner companions were well-traveled, discussing their travels around the world. She, on the other hand, had been in three states, Georgia and North and South Carolina. Not that she didn't want to travel. The opportunity just hadn't come up.

So where did that leave her with Morgan? She didn't know. She had committed herself to go with him to the Prescotts' party, but she wasn't looking forward to it.

The fact that he had dated Dianne Prescott was another thought that muddled her mind. Was that the kind of woman who interested him? He liked Marilyn as a friend, and she too oozed sophistication. How did a local girl measure up to that crowd?

Maybe going to the Prescotts' party was a good idea after all. There Callie could see exactly how the other half lived. Maybe it wouldn't be as bad as she thought. Certainly, Morgan didn't live the way she thought a singing star would. He attended church in Atlanta, although he hadn't found a church home in Highridge.

This Sunday he was going to her country church and eating dinner with her. But that was the day after the Prescott party. Would he still see her in the same light if she didn't fit in with his social set?

Callie turned off the light at last and crawled into bed. In her nightly talk with God, she asked for guidance in her relationship with Morgan. Within minutes she had fallen asleep and was surprised when the rooster announced that morning had come.

≈

Callie walked into the kitchen dressed in jeans, a short-sleeved shirt, and sneakers. "Morgan's coming to church with us Sunday," she told Grandma.

"Oh, he is?" Grandma nodded her head as though she weren't surprised. "You going to work like that?"

"Remember? Today is when I'm working at Seymour's ranch up north. I'll be home late. Bill Connell is going again this year. He knows more about farm equipment than I do."

This was Callie's second year to do a fiscal year-end report for Seymour's. Every tractor, every horse, every chicken had to be counted. It was outside work, and Callie was pleased Mr. Seymour had asked especially for her to work on his account. They had hit it off last year when Bill had taken her along to show her the ropes.

The day flew by as Callie and Bill counted and recorded everything on the ranch. Last year it was a two-day job, and it would be again. They quit at six and started the long drive back to Highridge. After a dinner at a fast-food hamburger place, they were back on the road, and Callie pulled onto her smooth-as-silk lane after nine o'clock.

She had told Morgan she'd be late on both Thursday and Friday, but now she wished she'd told him she would see him before the big event Saturday night.

In the privacy of her room, she put his compact disk on her portable player, her one extravagant purchase during her college days. His voice flowed through the earphones, but she pictured Trey singing, not Morgan. Maybe that was another thing that bothered her. Trey and Morgan were two different people to her. She needed to mesh the his two separate identities in her mind.

≥∘

The following day was a repeat of the first, except she and Bill finished their work at the ranch by four. By six-thirty she was home.

She hoped Morgan would call, but the clock ticked slowly toward bedtime, and the phone remained silent.

≥∘

By Saturday Callie was a nervous mess. She called Marilyn and learned the dress for the party would be casual. Callie decided on navy blue slacks, a cream-colored blouse, and a multi-colored patchwork vest. Grandma had made the vest out of different leftover fabrics and decorated it with beads, buttons, and ribbons. Callie had seen one similar in an exclusive Highridge dress shop, and Grandma had done a marvelous job of tailoring it.

Morgan arrived exactly at eight o'clock. The moment they drove out of sight of the house he stopped the car and leaned over and kissed her.

"I have missed you," he said. "I ended up flying to Kansas City to sit in on negotiations with the flight attendants. I flew back into Asheville exactly," he glanced at his watch, "three hours ago."

"Is the strike settled?" Callie asked. She'd been wondering why he hadn't called her. Now she knew.

"Settled before they walked out, which would have been at midnight tonight. We made a couple of concessions, but they made a couple, too. I think both sides came out feeling pretty good." He started the car again.

"Did your being a singer hamper negotiations?" Callie asked, remembering that he had voiced that reservation earlier.

"Actually," he said thoughtfully, "I think it helped. This sounds egotistical, but the attendants knew my music and were impressed that I was there. I hope they saw me as a business-man and not only a musician."

"Did anyone ask you to sing a number?"

"No," he said and laughed.

"Then I think you're safe. You can mix both careers."

"I hope so," he said. "Listen, about tonight. Vic's husband Adam is here. They're leaving in a couple days for Maine to visit his family. They'll be at the party. So will Mom."

"Good. I'd like to meet Adam."

"You'll like him. He's good to Vic. You'll see."

Morgan parked the car at his house and introduced Callie to his brother-in-law before they walked down the hill to the Prescotts'.

Victoria positively radiated love for her husband. He kept her arm tucked in his as they walked side by side. Every few steps he'd whisper something to her and she'd whisper back.

Dorothy walked beside Morgan and Callie. "Two weeks is a long time to be apart," she said, nodding toward the couple who walked ahead of them. "He's a good family man."

As the group neared the Prescotts', Callie was glad they

had walked down the mountain. Cars lined the road on both sides.

"Is this the social event of the season?" she asked.

"Not really. But any excuse to get together is a winner. There will be some interesting people here. You'll recognize some actors. You won't know some of the corporation presidents, but they're powerful people in the business world."

"I see." Morgan's words made her feel apprehensive. Year-rounders and summer folk don't mix; the expression she had heard all her life reared up in her mind, and her step faltered.

"Isn't that Robert and Marilyn?" Callie nodded toward a couple walking toward them.

"Yes. Robert's house is just around that curve. There are only a couple of houses between his and the Prescotts'."

They waited for the other couple to join them, then a maid admitted them to the house, and the group found themselves surrounded by party-goers. A young girl in a black caterer's uniform passed them with a tray loaded with hors d'oeuvres. She lowered the tray and Callie tried a tiny new potato topped with caviar. She didn't care for the taste.

Callie saw Dianne the moment they entered the massive great room. She looked like the reigning queen of the prom, smiling and nodding at her subjects, dressed in a form-fitting black, below-the-knee dress. The neckline was cut almost to her waist, and it had no back at all.

"I thought this was informal," Callie whispered to Marilyn.

"It is. Do you see anyone else dressed to kill?"

Marilyn wore a silk turquoise jump suit. Victoria was in a two-piece lounge set. Callie glanced down at her patchwork vest that had seemed so elegant an hour ago. Now it seemed to shout that it was homemade.

Morgan put his arm around Callie and escorted her further into the room.

Dianne looked up from the admiring males around her and straight at Callie. Her eyes lost their smile, although she kept one painted on her lips.

She made her way to Morgan's side and slipped her arm through his. "Trey, I'm so glad you could come. Good evening, Marilyn, Robert." She ignored Callie.

"You remember meeting Callie at the pool?" Morgan remarked, as if unaware of the cut to Callie, although his eyes relayed a different message.

"Why, yes. Callie." Dianne nodded to her.

"Good evening, Dianne. It's a lovely party."

"If you'll excuse us a moment, I have someone I want Trey to meet," she purred.

Morgan started to object, but Callie stopped him. "That's fine. I need to freshen up anyway. I'll see you in a few minutes." She turned to Marilyn and asked if she knew where the powder room was.

Marilyn led the way to a huge main floor rest room with a vanity area divided off from the toilet area by a louvered door.

"Sorry to drag you in here, but I didn't want to lose my temper with that woman. A retreat seemed the best course," Callie explained, examining her reflection in the mirror and willing the flush on her cheeks to go away.

"Don't pay any attention to Dianne. She's just jealous. She and Morgan used to date in the summers. Now that she's divorced, she wants to start it up again with Morgan. He's too smart for that. Besides, he's found you." She patted Callie on the arm. "Come on, let's go find Robert."

"Wait. What about you and Robert? Something's happened between you two."

Marilyn smiled. "He insisted on talking to my parents earlier this evening. Can you keep a secret?"

"Of course."

"Next week my parents are giving a party at the club house," she paused a moment, "to announce our engagement."

Callie hugged Marilyn. "Wow. Once he realized what you meant to him, he moved quickly."

"I know. We're getting married in August, and Robert's moving to New York. My work is there, and he can write anywhere. We'll keep the house here for summer vacations and weekends."

"You've got it all figured out."

"Yes. We've talked nonstop since the other night. I can't tell you how happy I am."

"You don't have to. It shows."

They rejoined the party and found Robert conversing with one of the Prescotts.

"Hi, P.J.," Marilyn greeted the man. "It's been a long time."

"You're all grown up, Marilyn. Last I remember you, you were a brat in pigtails." P.J. laughed and put his arm around Marilyn, but all the while he was staring at Callie.

"Callie, this is P.J. Prescott," Marilyn said. Before she completed the introduction, Morgan appeared, no Dianne tailing him now but with another man in tow instead.

"Callie, this is Phillip Anderson. He's been coming to the mountains for over forty years."

Callie gasped and turned questioning eyes to Morgan, who merely shrugged. She took a deep breath and extended her hand to Phillip, and he smiled down at her from well over six feet. He had to be in his late fifties or early sixties. She hadn't thought of her father as being that old. Hadn't Grandma said she thought he was twenty or so that summer? That would make him only forty-something now. Of course, people carried age differently. He might have been quite a bit older than Daisy at the time of their ill-fated love affair.

In the dim lighting, she couldn't make out the color of his

eyes. Were they the same shade of green as hers? Or were they hazel? Maybe the green eyes came from a grandparent. She vowed to read about genes and heredity.

"You must love the mountain to come back year after year," she forced herself to say casually.

"Yes. There's peace here. When I was young my mother brought us for the summer and Dad joined us on weekends. Now I come when I can. Two weeks here, another week there, and lots of weekends."

"Phillip," someone called to him and he excused himself to join another group.

"Callie?" Morgan pulled her away from the others. "I didn't mean to spring him on you like that. I've met him before, but I'd forgotten about him. What do you think?"

"I don't know. I didn't think of my father as that old."

"I didn't have a sense of him being the one we're looking for either, but you never know. I'll find out what I can about him."

He steered Callie to another corner and introduced her to a couple of actors whom Callie had seen on TV. She knew her mouth hung open, just like those teenagers who besieged Morgan in public, and she stuttered when she said hello. However, in a short time they put her at ease and she saw that they, too, were normal people just like Morgan. Maybe she had exaggerated the difference between summer people and those who lived in the mountains year-round.

He introduced her to their hostess, Elizabeth Prescott.

"It's a lovely party," Callie murmured.

A perfectly coiffed and made-up Mrs. Prescott merely nodded with a strained, "How do you do?" and moved on. Callie revised her earlier opinion. There *were* differences between year-rounders and summer folk.

Morgan escorted Callie around the room, introducing her

to others, but she couldn't remember all the names. She smiled automatically and said, she hoped, all the right things. Twice she caught Dianne watching her.

Marilyn and Robert joined them again and this time Marilyn initiated a trip to the powder room.

"Why is it women can't go to the rest room alone?" Robert shook his head at Morgan.

Marilyn waved her finger at Robert and laughed. "It's a female secret you'll never know."

As soon as they entered the large rest room, Marilyn went through the louvered door to the inner area, leaving Callie in front of the large vanity. She stared at her reflection and applied lipstick. A moment later Dianne opened the door.

"Well, well. If it isn't Trey's newest little flame."

"Hello, Dianne."

"Until tonight I thought you were with Robert. Silly of me. I should have realized Marilyn wouldn't let him get away so easily."

"Excuse me, Dianne." Callie snapped her purse shut and moved toward the door.

Dianne stepped in front of her.

"I understand you're from around here, Callie. You know, Trey's just using you for a summer dalliance. That's his style. I'm surprised he'd stoop to a little hillbilly, but he came to the mountains early this year and pickings must have been slim. Now that women on his own social level are here, you'll be yesterday's memory."

Her heart pounding in her chest, Callie stood rooted to the floor. Her first instinct was to strike back. Her second was to run.

She did both, saying with tight lips, "I refuse to lower myself to your social level, Dianne," before she flounced out of the bathroom. A quick glance around the great room didn't locate Morgan, so with a determined step, she headed for the front door.

Outside, she stood statue still on the front step, wondering what to do.

eleven

Callie followed the front walk to the street. She heard the door open behind her but didn't turn around.

"Callie." Marilyn's voice stopped her, and Callie waited for her to reach her. Marilyn put her arm around Callie's shoulder. "Stay here. I'll go get Morgan."

"No. I'm too mad and confused to see him right now."

"I heard it all through the door, but I couldn't get myself put together and out there before you were gone. Oh, that woman has nerve!"

They fell into step together and walked around the curve to Robert's house.

"Forget Dianne. Like I told you before, she's jealous."

Callie nodded in the dark, but her heart was torn in two. "Would you take me home, Marilyn? Tell Morgan that I'll see him tomorrow. I can't go back, and I'd rather be alone."

"All right, Callie, if that's what you want. But I think Morgan would rather see you himself." Callie shook her head vehemently, and Marilyn didn't pursue it. She motioned to the sleek sports car parked in Robert's drive. "Climb in."

Callie sat in the passenger seat, silent on the trip home, but her head was crowded with thoughts. She ran her hand over the luxurious upholstery. Everyone on the mountain drove a sports car, while she drove a pickup. Year-rounders and summer folk don't mix; the thought repeated itself over and over like a broken record. By the time they arrived at her house, Callie was feeling hurt as well as angry.

"Can Morgan call you?" Marilyn asked. "That is, if I can

keep him from marching over here?"

Callie leaned over and hugged Marilyn before getting out of the car. "Thank you for being such a good friend. I've only known you briefly, but I know you're a truly good person. And yes, please have Morgan call me. I owe him an explanation." With that she shut the door and walked to the front porch where Grandma had left the light on.

Grandma was already in bed, and Callie was glad. She didn't want to explain anything now. She carefully closed Grandma's bedroom door and sat down in the rocking chair beside the phone to wait for Morgan's call. She got up and turned off the porch light, then returned to the rocker to sit in the dark.

By instinct, she reached for the phone as it started to ring, picking it up before it had pierced the air with more than a sharp ping.

"Hello, Morgan," she said.

"What happened?" She could hear the scowl in his voice.

"Dianne and I had a disagreement," she said simply, "so I left."

"Why?"

"Because I'm not of her social standing. I believe the party was only for Regal Mountain dwellers."

"I'll be right over."

"No. Morgan, no. Grandma is already asleep, and I'm suddenly exhausted. I'll see you in the morning as we planned."

"Callie, I'm so sorry. I'll take care of it." He sounded menacing.

"Please, Morgan. It's over and I'm all right. Let's forget it. Okay?" she pleaded.

"I'll see you in the morning, Callie. Nine o'clock sharp. You did say you're fixing dinner for me after church, didn't you? I trust you're as good a cook as Grandma." His attempt at light chatter didn't conceal the sharp edge of steel in his voice.

"I'm a good cook," Callie said. "Good night, Morgan."

She hung up the receiver and sat in the dark awhile longer. Morgan wouldn't let the incident go unnoticed. But what he would do, she didn't know. She didn't want to be an embarrassment to him.

"Dear God, what do I do?" she whispered into the dark. "I know You teach forgiveness, but I need help with that. I know Dianne is hurting and wants love from Morgan—but I want love from him, too. Only is that enough? How can two different worlds work together? Please, Father, help me see the way."

Father. And what of her earthly father? In her heart she knew that Phillip Anderson wasn't the man. Wouldn't she have felt some sort of emotional pull if he'd been related to her?

What would her father look like now? Grandma had said he was pretty tall and had dark hair. That hair could be gray now, like Phillip Anderson's. Grandma had only guessed that he'd have green eyes. Still, Callie knew it was someone else.

She'd been rocking back and forth, back and forth, and finally forced herself to get ready for bed. With care, she hung up her homemade vest. Why had she let those people make her ashamed of it? Grandma had sewn each seam with loving care. Never again would she let summer people make her feel ashamed of her clothes or anything else.

She knew she was making generalizations about summer people. The Rutherfords had been more than kind to her, and she felt a special kinship with Marilyn and Robert. But did her father fit in the uppity class or the kind class?

So many unanswered questions. She crawled into bed and wished for morning—and was stunned when she opened her eyes to see the pink shades of dawn stream through the window.

She put on a pot of coffee before heading toward the shower. Rarely did she wake up earlier than Grandma, who usually lit a fire in the cook stove and started coffee in the old coffee-pot. Grandma said coffee tasted better when it was fixed the old-fashioned way, but Callie had invested in a drip coffee maker anyway. When she got out of the shower and into her robe, the coffee was ready without the fuss of feeding the fire.

Grandma was up and in the kitchen. Grumble as she might, she was drinking a cup of Callie's brew.

"How'd it go last night, Callie Sue? You was in pretty early." Grandma's shrewd eyes bored into Callie's. Callie sighed, knowing Grandma would have the truth and now.

Callie took a deep breath. "Dianne Prescott, who once dated Morgan, told me I was not of her social level."

"What did you do?"

"I didn't want to cause a scene, although I told her I wouldn't stoop to her social level. It was her house, so I held my head up high and walked out."

"And what did Morgan say?"

"He wasn't around, so I asked Marilyn, Robert's fiancee, to bring me home. Morgan called. You heard the phone?"

"Yes, but I couldn't make out the words," Grandma admitted.

"I have no idea what he said to Dianne, but I'll bet it wasn't pleasant. He wanted to come over, but I told him I was going to bed, and I'd see him today."

Callie got to her feet, not wanting to discuss Dianne Prescott any further. Instead, she scurried around and peeled potatoes and set them in water.

"What's for dinner, Callie Sue?"

"Pork chops, scalloped potatoes, spinach salad, applesauce,

and strawberry shortcake. Oh, and hot biscuits. Do you think we need some peas?"

Grandma gave her a sharp look. "Now don't go thinkin' you gotta put on airs for Morgan. We're plain folk, Callie Sue. He has to want you the way you are. You can't be something you ain't," she admonished with a wave of her index finger.

"You're right, Grandma. But did you ever fix dinner for Grandpa when you were dating?"

Grandma paused for a moment. "I see what you're tryin' to say, Callie Sue, and I guess it don't hurt none to fix somethin' special for company once in a while. I'll go pick some spinach. You sure you don't want to boil it?"

"I'm sure."

Together the women made as many early preparations for dinner as they could, then dressed for Sunday School.

Morgan arrived exactly at nine. He joined the two women for coffee in the kitchen and apologized to both of them for the events of the night before.

"What did you do, Morgan?" Callie asked.

"Rob and I waited for you and Marilyn. When you didn't come, we started looking around. Dianne told me you had a headache and had gone home, but we didn't buy that. We walked to Rob's house and discovered Marilyn's car gone, so we waited there until she returned. Then we went back to thank Mr. Prescott for inviting us, and we left. And so did half the party. There was pretty much a mass exodus, even though many of the guests didn't know why they were leaving early. I guess they figured it was the avant-garde thing to do. So, the Mountain had an early night." He laughed.

The trio finished their coffee and loaded into Morgan's van for the ride to Sunday School. Morgan was surprised at the dilapidated condition of the old church. From his view high on Regal Mountain he had seen it many times, the tall, sharp steeple a landmark. From a distance it appeared pristine white, but up close, multiple cracks in the stucco gave the structure a gray look.

"We have a building fund," Callie said, reading his expressive eyes. "We may put up a metal building and tear this down."

"A metal church? When was this built?"

"I don't know."

Grandma went inside while Callie and Morgan walked the perimeter of the building, looking for a cornerstone. They couldn't find one.

"We'll ask at the Sunday School meeting."

"Meeting?"

"We only have about fifty members, so we meet as a group, then break into classes."

Morgan hadn't seen anything like it. Inside the church, a wide aisle separated two rows of antique wooden pews. Morgan mentally measured the large room by counting ceiling beams and adding up the water-stained distance between them. He guessed fifty feet by twenty-five feet. The interior walls were wood, not cheap paneling, but tongue-in-groove wooden boards. A large gas heater sat at one side of the back door, the only entrance to the church. He imagined the stove had replaced a wood-burning one.

An old man of about eighty years pounded a gavel on an old podium. From his front pew seat, Morgan could see the square-headed nails that held the podium together.

The meeting began with the reading of the minutes of last week and the treasurer's report. Callie reported the building fund had one thousand, five hundred, and ninety-two dollars in it.

"We need to hold a pie supper or something to raise money

for the new building," the old man said. "We're years away from getting a new place."

Callie raised her hand. "How old is this building?" she asked.

"Built in eighteen-aught-four," he answered without hesitation. "Been updated a few times."

"Is it possible to restore it?" Morgan whispered to Callie.

"Can we fix it up instead of tearing it down?" she asked. "It's such a pretty place. Have any of you been down to Mt. Shira and looked at their new metal building? It's bigger all right, and has rooms for Sunday School, but we don't have that kind of membership."

"No, missy, but we need something that will stand up. I think we'd all rather have this place fixed, but it needs big repairs."

"What we need," Grandma said, "is a bigger money-maker than a pie supper." She cast a sly look at Morgan, who sat beside her. "What we need is a big-name singer to star in a tent show."

Callie gasped. How dare Grandma put Morgan on the spot like that.

"You happen to know anybody like that?" the old man asked, unknowingly putting Morgan in his place.

"Yep. This here fellow is a singer by the name of Trey." Muffled squeals were heard from the seven or eight teenage girls present. "He'd draw a big crowd. We just need to advertise. I'll bet we could make ten thousand dollars in one night, if we had a big enough tent."

"I take it you kids have heard of this Trey?" the old man said and pointed at Morgan.

Morgan felt his face flush. He'd been so relieved when his last tour was over, and he'd made the firm decision that he wouldn't perform live again. He didn't mind studio work or even the videos he shot for music TV stations, but live work was different. "What do you say, young fellow?" the elderly man asked.

He would have to call the musicians up to the mountains. He could have a house-party, though, for his family would be gone in another few days. Even if the church scheduled the benefit for after his return to Atlanta, he could come up for the night and certainly the weekend.

"You don't have to do this," Callie whispered.

Morgan glanced at Grandma. "Yes, I do," he whispered back. "She's asked me. I can't turn her down."

He stood up. "I'll be glad to headline a performance," he said, "on the condition that the money raised be used to renovate this building instead of tearing it down and replacing it with a metal building. There's too much history here to let it be destroyed."

The meeting continued with a quick vote for keeping the old church. A committee was set up to look into how much it would cost to replace the roof and the windows, re-stucco the outside, and get a bigger heating system.

Callie and Grandma were put on the committee for the tent show. Four others were selected to help, including two teenagers, even though all of them had volunteered.

The meeting adjourned and the group broke into Sunday School classes. Morgan went with Callie to the back left of the room. Three other singles joined them, and Callie opened her quarterly and shared it with Morgan.

"Anger is one letter short of danger," the leader, Jean Rogers, read. "I've heard that all my life," she said, "and I believe it. The Bible has taught us to turn the other cheek, and we've been taught to hold our tongue when in an argument. But do we all do that?"

"I think we have to stick up for ourselves, too," Tommy

Ray spoke up. "I know the meek shall inherit the earth, but isn't there a point where we should be heroes instead of wimps?"

"I think we have to stand up for what we believe in," Callie said. "There are lots of ways to interpret 'meek.' Meek can mean obedient. And our obedience is to God, not to those who would lead us astray."

The others agreed and the discussion continued. Callie thought back to last night when she had walked out of the Prescott home. The best route would have been silence, but she had gotten in her one barb first.

"What we need to learn is tolerance for others' opinions," Morgan was saying. "We're not to judge others' behavior, but we're to be in control of our own. So when others make us angry, we have to choose which course of action is best. Stand up to that person or walk away."

"But we have to decide," Jean inserted. "We shouldn't let the other person force us into a quick decision. My dad told me long ago that we didn't have to do anything—except live with our choices."

Thirty minutes later, the old man who had presided over the Sunday School rang a hand bell and Jean tied up the discussion. Morgan and Callie moved back to the front of the church and sat by Grandma. When the song leader called out the first selection, the small congregation stood and sang "The Old Rugged Cross."

Callie and Morgan each held a side of the song book. Her soft soprano mixed with his rich tenor. She loved his voice, and for the first time, hearing him sing the hymn, she connected Morgan and Trey as one.

"Peace in the Valley," and "In the Sweet By and By" completed the singing portion of the worship service. The old man read from the Bible, offered a prayer, and dismissed the congregation.

"No sermon?" Morgan asked, as they made their way toward the back door.

"Only every other Sunday. We share a minister with another church. We don't have weekly preaching, but we do gather to worship."

"That's what church is for," Morgan said.

Outside, several people gathered around Callie and Morgan, waiting for introductions. The teenagers, with awe-filled eyes, shook Morgan's hand.

"I saw you in Asheville four years ago," one girl said. "I can't believe you're here," she squealed.

When they were finally back at Callie's house, she swung into action in the kitchen.

"What can I do?" Morgan asked.

"Just sit and talk to me," Callie answered and fed kindling into the big stove. She mixed white sauce as they discussed the tent show.

Morgan helped Grandma set the table. Callie glanced over and saw Grandma was using the good dishes, the ones they had gotten many years ago at a service station with each fill-up. Rarely did Grandma think the occasion warranted the good dishes, and Callie couldn't suppress a grin as she caught Grandma's eye.

Grandma gave a sniff and a look that said, "Don't say a word about it."

twelve

Morgan had to take some action to find Phillip. He had thought of hiring a detective, but Callie had nixed that idea. A detective might arouse too many suspicions, asking questions and all. She wasn't ready for Grandma to know anything about her search.

Morgan didn't know where to turn. He could hardly go door to door asking who had owned each house twenty-four years ago. He didn't even know who had owned his house back then. He needed some advice from a detective.

Sinclair—that's who he needed. Robert's fictional detective.

He picked up the phone in his office and punched in Robert's number. The answer had been staring him in the face. Robert had taken classes in police procedures so his mysteries would be realistic. He could count on his friend to help him. He knew he could.

The phone rang four times, then the machine answered.

"Pick it up, Robert. I know you're there, and I need your help," he said as soon as he heard the beep.

"How do you know I'm here?" Robert answered. "And what kind of help do you need, Morgan?"

"I need Sinclair to solve a mystery. Can I come over?"

"Give me thirty minutes to finish this section. Front door's open."

Morgan read some letters that had been faxed earlier, called his office, and dictated responses. Then he called his manager.

"You're going to what?" Harry's voice was so loud that Morgan moved the receiver away from his ear and switched to the speaker phone. If Harry was going to yell, at least Morgan didn't have to hear his voice directly in his ear.

"It's not a full-fledged concert," Morgan told his manager one more time. "No warm-up act. Just me. I'll sing for an hour or so. It's a benefit performance. Aren't you the one who wanted me to get back in the public eye?"

"Couldn't you have picked a big charity so you could get more publicity out of this? Once you start doing this stuff free, every little cause will call me up. Will he do this? Will he do that?"

"That's why I pay you the big bucks, Harry. To handle that sort of thing. The benefit is a week from Saturday night. Are you coming up?"

"I suppose I'll have to," he growled. "How many musicians do you need?"

As soon as he finished with the details, Morgan walked down the mountain to Robert's and let himself in the front door.

"Coffee's on," Robert called from his office. "Be just a minute."

Morgan poured coffee into a china cup and smiled to himself. Robert was more the mug sort, but he had bought the house furnished and had not seen the need to personalize anything in it. Now, seeing Robert with a fine china cup and saucer in his hand seemed natural.

"Okay," Robert said as he entered the kitchen. "What's the mystery?"

"I can't tell you everything. I mean, I can tell you all I know, but I can't tell you why I need to know."

Robert picked up a pad of paper and pencil from the counter and sat down at the table. "Start from the beginning," he said.

"I need to find the full name of a man called Phillip who lived on Regal Mountain twenty-four years ago. A least in the summers. Or maybe in town. He's tall and had dark hair back then. Now he could be anywhere from forty-three to fifty something."

Robert looked puzzled. "You want to know the last name of a man called Phillip who lived here or in town twenty-four years ago?"

"That's right. How can we find him?"

"If he lived on Regal Mountain, we might find out from Billy."

Morgan hit his head with his palm. Of course. He should have thought of the caretaker. Billy might have records from the time Regal Mountain was first developed. "Let's go," Morgan said.

"Not so fast. You can't tell me why?"

"No. At least not yet. And could you pretend you're doing research for a book? Maybe checking out a procedure your detective would use?"

Robert nodded.

"I owe you one. Hey, you want free tickets to a concert I'm giving for Callie's church?" Morgan explained about the upcoming tent show.

"You've got it bad," Robert said and shook his head.

❧

"He's got it bad," Marilyn said, when Callie called her for advice about the tent show.

Callie had a half-hour between client meetings and had worked on a schedule of details necessary for the concert.

"I don't know about that. My grandmother put him on the spot. What could he do?"

"He could have said 'no.' It's a simple word."

Callie laughed. "I suppose he could have, but he said he'd

do it. But getting back to why I called—have you ever put on an event that needed publicity?"

"Not what you're needing. The functions I've had to organize had a guest list. What you need to do is find out the fastest way to get the word out. Radio and TV ads would work. But you have a small budget, don't you?"

"No budget. I checked on tent rental, and our tent show is now an evening under the stars."

"How about lunch, Callie? I'll work on some ideas and we'll go over them."

By lunchtime, Callie had worked on a list of her own, and she and Marilyn put their heads together over a pizza.

"Most important thing is publicity," Marilyn said. "If people don't know about it, they can't come. With no money, you can't advertise unless you barter. We give the radio so many tickets to give away. The same with the TV station."

Callie was glad to hear Marilyn use "we," as if she were going to work on this project. "Closest TV station is Asheville," she said.

"That's okay. People from here go to Asheville to shop and for concerts. Nothing says people from Asheville won't come to Highridge to hear Trey, who hasn't given a concert in two years. He's got it bad." Marilyn chuckled. "I'm leaving tomorrow, but I'll be back on Friday to help with the engagement party. I'm arranging for the next week off so Mom and I can plan the wedding. Here's my number in New York. If you need anything before I get back, call. We've got to move on this. Get tickets printed today."

"Impossible. I've got to get back to work," Callie said.

"Then I'll take care of it. Give me the details."

"The committee is meeting tonight at my house. We'll have to decide all that then. Want to come? Oh, sorry. It's your last night with Robert."

"I'll be there with Robert in tow. He might have some good ideas, too."

Callie gulped down a last bite of pizza and rushed out the door. She wished she didn't have a full afternoon calendar, but that couldn't be helped. She'd have to have some time off to do all the running around this concert required. She'd probably make a trip to Asheville to deliver tickets once they were printed, unless she could con someone else into doing that.

Don't worry until you have something to worry about, she told herself. One day at a time. This will get done.

ə

Billy flipped through an old log book until he found the right year. "You just want a guy named Phillips?"

"No, his first name was Phillip. I don't know the last name," Robert said.

Morgan stood behind him in the guardhouse and shifted for a better view. Billy wasn't letting them take the book, but said he'd look up the information for Robert. Morgan moved to Billy's other side and stared at the book on the counter.

They'd come down that morning to discover Billy had gone to town. Because of the card system, Billy wasn't bound to the guard house all day. The residents liked having him visible, since it was double security, but they didn't complain when he occasionally left his post. After lunch, they had checked the guard house again and found him.

"Now tell me again why you want this?"

"Just checking a procedure. My character has this same problem to solve. I just wondered how easy it would be to locate someone from the past with only a first name and a brief description."

"I read one of your books," Billy said. "Got it from the library. That Sinclair knows what he's doing. Do you check out all his problems like this?"

"Most of them. That's the log?" Robert pointed to the old ledger that lay open.

"Yep." Billy read down the row, using his finger as a guide. "Phillip Anderson lived here then. His folks had the house. He inherited it."

"You have all the kids' names here, too?" Morgan asked.

"Sure. Had to know which kids to let in. We've only had this card system on the gates for the last ten years."

Billy ran his finger down the row of names. Morgan watched as he turned to another page. "Here's Phillip Bartlett. He doesn't live here anymore. Sold that house to the Sheldons about fifteen years ago."

"And how old was Phillip Bartlett?" Robert asked as he wrote the name down in what Morgan called his clue note-book, since he always carried it with him in case he got an idea for a plot.

"I don't know. Seems like he was a young fellow. Inherited his dad's oil business. See, just the wife and one kid listed with him." He looked up in the air to search his memory. "Yeah, they had a baby when he lived here."

Billy returned his attention to the list and turned another page. "Phillip Baker. Had three boys and one was Phillip Baker, Junior. I remember them. They sold the place at the end of that summer. See, I entered another family right next to their names."

Morgan stared at the name. Phillip Baker, Junior. This had to be the Phillip he was looking for. Since he had moved from Regal Mountain, he couldn't have returned and found that Daisy had borne his child.

"That's it. No more Phillips. You want to try another name? Maybe Sinclair could look for somebody with a real strange name and find it on the first look," Billy suggested.

"No, this is fine," Robert said. "I can't make it too easy for him. I'll have him check out each Phillip. Do you have addresses for these Phillips?"

"Might not be any good any more, that being so long ago and all. People sure move a lot these days. Now, the wife and I have been here at the foot of Regal going on thirty years. Never moved a step."

Robert wrote down the addresses, and then back at Robert's house, Morgan copied the information from the small spiral notebook.

"What makes you think it's Phillip Baker?" Robert asked as he put on another pot of coffee.

"Did I say I did?"

"You looked like it. Is it important that he moved? Why couldn't it be Phillip Bartlett? The age could be right."

Morgan drummed his fingers on the kitchen table and considered what he could tell Robert without breaking his word to Callie. "He had an affair with a local girl," he said at last. "A summer fling. And he never came back."

"Maybe he came back. Maybe he just didn't look the girl up again. Did she check to see that he wasn't here?"

"No," Morgan replied. Robert was obviously getting into Sinclair's character now and was asking too many questions.

"Why not? And why can't she tell you his last name? Did he lie about it or not tell her at all?"

"She's dead. She died before he returned the following summer, if he did return."

"The plot thickens." Robert turned around from the cabinet where he'd returned the coffee canister. "Murdered?"

Morgan took a deep breath. "She died in childbirth."

Robert had a sudden understanding in his eyes, and Morgan knew he had said too much. "And now the child wants to find her father," Robert said. "I'll help anyway I can."

thirteen

By seven o'clock, the committee members plus Morgan, Marilyn, and Robert were sipping lemonade in Callie's living room. With the organizational skills known to CPAs, Callie checked off the items on the list one by one as the committee made decisions.

"Outside is fine," Morgan said, "but I'll need a raised platform."

"Will a flatbed truck be enough room? We could probably get two. That would make it double wide." At Morgan's okay, Dick Menner wrote that chore on his list.

If all tasks were divided up, this wouldn't be too much trouble, Callie thought.

"We're going to need rest rooms," Marilyn mentioned. "We'll have to rent the portable kind, but we'll need a row of them."

"Do you think we could use the building fund as seed money for this project?" Callie asked the other adult committee members.

They decided they'd have to ask at Sunday School for approval. Meanwhile, they could go ahead and schedule rental for the portable rest rooms.

"What about a sound system?" one of the two teens asked. Both girls stared awestruck at Morgan, barely moving their gazes away from him to enter into the discussion.

"I'll take care of that," Morgan said.

"We should fence off the area," Dick said, "or we'll have people come in without paying.

"We'll need security of some sort," Morgan said. He remembered the second concert on his last tour. He had been pulled off stage by fans who just wanted to touch him. "But I can take care of that, too." He'd have Harry bring security guards from Atlanta. He'd put them up in motels for the night. Harry would squawk about it, since it would be more expense out of Morgan's pocket, but Callie wouldn't know that it wasn't something he provided for every concert. It'd be one less thing for her to be concerned with.

By nine o'clock the meeting broke up. Callie had checked off all her items, and Marilyn had gone through her list, too. She had called printers, checked prices, and arranged for Callie to take ticket information in early the next morning. The printer had guaranteed her he'd have the tickets done by Wednesday noon.

Morgan lingered after the others had gone.

"Would it help if I went with you to the TV and radio stations?" he asked Callie.

"Are you serious? They'd want interviews and all. Are you willing to do that?"

"No problem. Harry will say it'll be good publicity. Walk me to the car, Callie?"

Outside, he slipped his arm around her shoulder and placed her arm around his waist as they walked to the sports car. He explained what he'd found out about Phillip and how he'd done his research.

"Although I didn't tell him, Robert pieced together why I'm trying to find Phillip." He hadn't wanted to tell her, but he didn't want to keep secrets from her. He wanted their relationship based on trust.

Callie was quiet for a long moment. "What did he say?"

"He said he'd help anyway he could."

"He's a good friend."

"The best. You can trust him."

Callie smiled and in the dimness of dusk, her expression seemed to Morgan like the sun coming out from behind a cloud.

"What's next? How can you trace these Phillips?"

"I'm not sure, but I'll let you know the minute we find out anything." He drew her into his arms, and she rested her head on his chest.

If only she could stay there forever. After he kissed her goodnight, she reluctantly let him go.

ða

The next morning Callie arrived at work an hour early and drew up a sample ticket on her computer. She transferred it to a disk and drove to the printer's. Returning to work, she focused on the most pressing problems and arranged to take Wednesday afternoon off.

Callie called radio and TV stations, lining up interviews. She explained the interview agenda to Morgan that night when she went to his house for dinner. She bid farewell to Victoria's family, as they were leaving the next morning for a week in Maine.

"We'll be back for your concert," Vic promised Morgan.

Dorothy was also leaving the next day for Alaska. "Just a little trip with Mary. We're going to take a boat from Seattle. But we'll fly back for your concert, Morgan."

Callie was amazed that they took flying for granted. When money was no object, she guessed one could be almost anywhere at a moment's notice. For someone who had been in only three states, that was a revelation and another reminder that the Duncans and the Rutherfords lived in two very different worlds.

ða

Wednesday morning Callie again went into the office early.

She darted to the printers at ten-thirty after they called and said the tickets were ready.

"I'll be back in ten minutes," she told Liz, then agreed to pick up some paper coffee cups for the office.

The tickets looked great. She ran into the grocery store on her way back to the office and was standing in the express line when she glanced at the tabloids and froze. Trey smiled at her on the cover—and her own face was looking up at him with love in her eyes.

"Superstar Trey with This Summer's Love at Secret Mountain Hideaway."

She grabbed every copy of the tabloid in the rack and as soon as she'd paid the checker, she ran for the car.

The picture had been taken the night at Murphy's. The man with the camera who had snapped photos of the Prescott family reunion had taken hers with Morgan. She remembered him taking a picture of the Prescott girls with Morgan, but this shot was taken without her knowledge.

She fumbled through pages until she found the story. It was only two columns and contained little information. It didn't mention the town's name, but her name was printed three times. "Is this the love who's keeping him away from his adoring fans?"

"No," she said aloud.

If she'd doubted Morgan before when he'd told her tabloids made up their news, she now knew it for a fact. She stared at the picture again, then started the car.

An unexpected client was waiting when she got back to the office. He stood beside Liz, looking at the same tabloid on Liz's desk.

"You won't believe what Sarah found on her coffee break," Liz exclaimed.

"I think I would," Callie said through a forced smile. She

realized the futility of buying out the rack. She hadn't even hit the other checkout aisles at the grocery store. Besides, every convenience store and the other grocery stores would have them.

"Can you imagine being linked with Trey? Why, millions of people will know your name, Callie."

"Yes. My fifteen minutes of fame will be on the front page of a tabloid." She turned to her client, dismissing the article as though it had no importance, but inside she was cringing. "Good to see you, John. Shall we go back to my office?"

Callie plunked the coffee cups on Liz's desk and escorted John down the hallway. As soon as she pulled out his file, she focused her thoughts away from the article and onto John's questions on his fiscal year-end report.

But when John left, her mind returned to the picture and she wondered who had given it to the tabloid. She thought the man with the camera at Murphy's had been one of the Prescott sons. Why would he send the photo to the tabloid?

Dianne. Of course. She would know that Callie wouldn't want this sort of innuendo cast on her. Would she be this devious? Wouldn't she think Morgan would hold it against her, too?

But Morgan didn't take this stuff seriously. He said it was publicity and people didn't believe it. Callie hated to differ with him, but lots of people believed whatever they saw in print. She would have to show Grandma and convince her the headline wasn't true. Callie wasn't a summer fling for Morgan.

Or was she? her dark side argued.

No. He had been going to profess his love the very night that photo was taken.

But he hadn't said anything since, and he'd had the opportunity.

She pushed the argument to the back of her mind and answered Liz's buzz. Then she settled down with her next client.

She scurried home exactly at noon and showed Grandma the tabloid as she gulped down a sandwich. Morgan arrived for her a half-hour later. He seemed ill at ease and stood by the front door.

"Oh, Callie," he paused for a moment searching for the right words. "There's a story. . ."

"I read it," Callie said. She had wanted to talk to him about the tabloid and was glad he had brought it up.

"I read it, too," Grandma piped up. Morgan noticed the frown line on her forehead. For every step forward in his relationship with the old woman, he seemed to take two steps back.

"I don't know who sent that in, but I had nothing to do with it. I was surprised when Harry, my manager, called me about it. It's not true, of course."

Grandma lifted her eyebrows.

"It's true that I'm seeing Callie," he quickly added. "I mean the summer love thing isn't true." Grandma's expression had darkened, and Morgan blurted, "Not that I don't love Callie." He glanced at Callie and saw her wide eyes. "Just the summer thing. It's not a summer thing. I mean, I know it's summer, but it's. . ." He stopped mid-sentence. This stammering was not how he intended to tell Callie that he loved her. "What I mean is, I had nothing to do with it. Tabloids make up items all the time."

"They say where there's smoke, there's fire," Grandma said.

"Sometimes the smoke is as simple as a dinner date," Morgan said. "The fire was invented from the writer's imagination. Occasionally writers might be on target, but likely as not, they add two and two and get thirteen."

"I believe you, Morgan," Grandma said. "All you had to tell me was you didn't know anything about it."

He glanced at Callie.

"Me, too," she said.

He let out a big breath without realizing he'd been holding it. "Okay. Good." He led her out to his car to begin their publicity rounds.

That afternoon, Callie met Trey.

The man she spent the day with was the superstar, the singer who charmed his audiences. The reception at the radio station in Highridge further merged Morgan's and Trey's identities in her mind. By the time they arrived in Asheville at the television station, she was in awe of him.

"You're a split personality," she told him as they waited in the newsroom for an on-camera interview. The news anchor had jumped at the chance to talk to Trey on the air.

"No," he protested. "I'm Morgan Rutherford the Third who happens to be a singer. Singing is part acting. The public expects me to be a little bigger than life, and I try to fit the image they've given me."

"Well, Trey. . ."

"Don't call me Trey," he interrupted. "I'm Morgan to you." He paused. "I guess I am split. But I don't want my friends to think of me as a performer. I want them to think of me as a plain man."

Callie laughed, a high tinkling sound. "I would never describe you as a plain man. Morgan is more approachable than Trey, so you'll always be Morgan to me. But I think you're about to become Trey again." She pointed to the newsman, who was waving to him through the glass.

The door to the on-air room opened and the anchor popped out. "We're ready for you. We have two minutes of commercials, then we're on. You'll sit in the weatherman's chair."

Morgan took a seat at the news desk while a technician affixed a mini-microphone to his shirt collar and strung the wire behind him.

Callie watched from behind the glass window of the news-room. Behind Morgan was a large photo of downtown Asheville framed in a window setting to give the illusion of being the view from the on-camera news desk.

The cameraman held up his hand and closed each finger as he counted. "In five, four, three, two, one." He pointed at the anchor.

"A surprise guest wandered off the streets of Asheville to-day. Vacationing in the mountains, Trey, four-time Grammy winner, has agreed to do a benefit performance in Highridge a week from Saturday. We'll be giving away tickets to his concert. Details on that at the end of the newscast. Now, Trey, our viewers would like to know when your next album will be released."

"I'm writing songs for it now. So it will probably be out in December. I thought I'd try a couple of the numbers on the audience in Highridge."

"How are you inspired? Do you have to be in a certain mood to write a song? Does a woman inspire the love songs?"

Morgan glanced at Callie. "A woman helps," he said and nodded.

"Although our viewers can't see her, I believe you brought with you the same woman who shared the cover of this week's *Inquirer*. Care to comment?"

Morgan laughed easily. "Isn't the standard comment 'just friends'? For now I'll stick with that."

Callie felt heat on her face and ducked away from the glass. She watched the rest of the interview on the small screen TV in the newsroom, marveling at how real the set looked on the TV and how phony it looked in reality.

At the next commercial, Morgan came out the door.

"Do you have the tickets?"

Callie pulled the envelope marked with the station's call letters and address out of her purse. "Ten tickets. Think that's enough?"

"Sure. We want others to buy them. Is the list of purchase places in here?"

Callie nodded. Liz had made calls for her earlier, lining up music stores in each town for ticket sales.

After delivering tickets to another TV station, taping an interview there, since it was after the live newscast, and delivering tickets to music stores, they stopped for dinner.

"We're probably forgetting something major," Callie said over a slab of barbecued ribs.

"I'll talk to Harry tomorrow and have him fax me a list of details he takes care of for each performance. He may have something we haven't thought of. If we forget anything, he'll be there for the concert and can help us out."

"I can't believe you're doing this. Are you feeling apprehensive?"

"Getting scared, you mean? The thought crosses my mind at night. I've dreamed I've forgotten the words."

"You won't. All you have to do is have faith that God will help you with your show. And I know He will help you raise our building fund. You might say He has a stake in this performance."

"You're right. I pray for help before I ever walk out on stage. And I'm preparing. I practiced my new songs this morning, memorizing the words, and I'll rehearse with the band when I go back to Atlanta next week."

Callie looked down at the ribs and knew she couldn't eat another bite now that he had mentioned that his vacation was nearing an end.

"You've been working every day, haven't you?"

"I call my office and check in. I'm not out of touch, but it's different being there to check with the presidents of each company. There's a personal touch that's missing when I'm out of town."

"I suppose." Callie moved her food around on her plate, then looked up at him. "I don't want you to go," she blurted.

Morgan smiled. "Good. But I'll be back—a lot. Atlanta's only a couple of hours away."

❧

The rest of his vacation time sped by.

Saturday night Marilyn and Robert's engagement party was a huge success. The only blot on it for Callie was the appearance of Dianne Prescott and her family. Marilyn had warned her in advance that the Prescotts had been invited.

"My mother wanted the entire mountain invited. To exclude the Prescotts might cause hard feelings among some of their neighbors. The Prescotts have been here a long time."

Marilyn glowed with love and Robert kept a possessive arm around his fiancee.

"I'll be here until August," he told Morgan. "Then we'll live mainly in New York. But there will always be summers here in the mountains."

Sunday morning in the Sunday School meeting, Callie reported on the open-air concert and the progress that had been made.

"Although we'll sell tickets at the gate, we'll have a pretty good idea of advanced sales before then. We need ticket takers and parking attendants. We're going to use the two fields on the left side of the road adjacent to the field where we'll have the concert." She continued with the committee report and got approval to spend building fund money to pay for ticket printing and bathroom rentals.

After church, which let out late since they had a preacher this Sunday, Morgan took Grandma and Callie into Highridge for Sunday buffet at Holliman's fish camp.

"It's Grandma's favorite," Callie had told him. "She's never been to the ocean, but she loves fried clams."

After dinner, the trio returned to Eagle Mountain and Morgan suggested he and Callie take a hike up the mountain.

"We need to work off all those clams," he said.

"Maybe I'd better come, too," Grandma said with a grin and then she burst out laughing. "You should see the look on your face, Morgan. Go on, you two. Git."

They took off on the trail, pushing aside the scrub brush and vines that blocked their way. Mixed in with the dense woods were the ever present wild flowers adding their blues, yellows, oranges, and reds to the green ground cover. The clear blue sky that peeked through the branches above them promised a perfect day.

A perfect day except that Morgan was leaving for Atlanta that afternoon.

They climbed for half an hour, then stopped where the trail turned north.

"If you look through the foliage you can make out one of the houses on Regal," Callie said. "Regal's a lot higher than Eagle. That's how it got its name. It's the tallest around for at least fifteen miles."

"So, this is how your mother hiked over to Regal."

"I suppose so."

"This would make a good spot for a house. Look at the view." Callie murmured agreement as Morgan pulled her into his arms. "I need to be heading back to Atlanta," he said reluctantly.

"I know." Her voice was muffled since she had rested her head on his chest, her favorite place in the whole world.

"I'll be back on Thursday. Harry's coming up then, plus the band will be here Friday. I'll call you when we get here, and we'll plan on doing something that night. Okay?"

She nodded, but didn't look up. She found comfort in his arms.

He put his finger under her chin and lifted her face, then leaned down and kissed her. Three times.

"We'd better go back," he said. "Grandma may meet us at the foot of the mountain."

They made their way slowly back down the mountain, walking arm in arm where the path allowed, Morgan taking the lead when the path narrowed and holding Callie's hand behind him.

At the house he declined to go in for a cold drink. "I'd better go on." He kissed her again, and Callie kissed him back.

"God be with you," she said.

"And with you," he echoed. He blew her a kiss as he drove away.

fourteen

Back in Atlanta, Morgan called Pete, his arranger, and confirmed that he could get "Callie's Song" finished before Thursday. Morgan drove across the city and delivered the melody and words Sunday night. Pete said he'd have the drum, guitar, and violin parts done within a couple of days. Normally, Morgan wanted his musicians to rehearse a new song many times before they tried it on an audience, but this song was special, and he intended to sing it Saturday night.

Work at the corporate offices fell into a routine for the four days he was there. He found he'd kept well abreast of business while in the mountains, and as a result, he felt confident he could slip off for many three day weekends, if not an entire week here and there, during the summer. For as long as it took to court Callie, he would be going regularly to the mountains. For courting was exactly what he was doing, and he was courting two women, Callie and Grandma.

He also had to find Phillip. He and Robert had agreed that a private detective could be called in now that there were names to be traced. Although Robert had spent several hours at the library, flipping through large city phone books searching for Phillip Baker Junior, he had conceded that he didn't have the time to continue. He needed to finish his manuscript before his August wedding. Besides he could be on a wild goose chase. He might not pick the right city, and Baker could have an unlisted number.

On Monday Morgan hired a detective. By Tuesday afternoon he had a report on Phillip Baker Junior, age thirty-two, now residing in Memphis. He would have been eight that summer twenty-four years ago.

Morgan had been so sure that it was Baker, but he gave the detective Bartlett's name. By Thursday afternoon when Morgan left for the mountains, the detective hadn't located Phillip Bartlett, but would call Morgan in Highridge if he found him.

៛

Callie's week dragged by. She had plenty to do with the final arrangements for the concert, but she missed Morgan. Word of mouth spread the news that Trey was performing, and Joe from Franklin called Callie to make sure it was true.

"He's doing it for you," Joe said. "I'll be there. Anything I can do to help?"

"I'll have a job waiting for you," Callie answered. "Come by the house Saturday afternoon. The concert isn't until eight, but I know we'll have all sorts of last minute emergencies."

On Tuesday Callie received calls from three music stores for more tickets. She had more printed and dispatched the teens to deliver them. At fifteen dollars a ticket, they were hoping to reach more people, but the numbers were staggering. What about the number who would buy tickets at the gate?

Seating was spelled out on the tickets—bring a lawn chair or a blanket. Still the public wanted to see Trey in person.

She called the radio stations and told them to remind people to car pool to the concert as parking was limited. Dick Menner's fallow farm land was the site of the event. Callie called him and they decided on an additional field for parking.

"Let's hope it doesn't rain," Dick said.

"It's not goin' to rain," Grandma said when Callie confided her fears about the weather. "The good Lord will see to that."

Morgan called Tuesday night and told Callie that one of

the Phillips had been eliminated. "It could be that the other one isn't him either. We may have to widen the search to include Highridge." He told her he missed her and that he would see her Thursday evening.

Callie counted the minutes.

&

Thursday afternoon at two, Morgan ducked out of the office and ran to his car, his heart light. He'd see Callie in a few hours. He grinned at his reflection as he checked his rear-view mirror and backed out of his parking space.

The band would be arriving the next morning and all equipment should be there now. He'd given Harry a key to his house and told him to make himself at home and have the sound equipment unloaded in the garage.

The drive north seemed longer than normal and traffic was fairly heavy. City dwellers heading out of town for the week-end, he decided, getting an early start like himself.

He arrived home in time to say hi to Harry and picked up the phone. He dialed Callie's work number and waited while Liz connected him with her extension.

"I have missed you," he told her as soon as she picked up.

"Me, too," Callie said. "And I've heard your name every time I turn around. Liz is beside herself about the concert and has volunteered hours and hours making calls and running errands."

"Can you come to the house after work? We'll have dinner with Harry."

At five, Callie flew to Regal Mountain. As soon as she parked in his drive, Morgan was out the door and pulled her into his arms. He kissed her soundly.

"It's been a long week," he said.

"I know. And this is only Thursday," she said as they walked arm-in-arm into the house.

Morgan introduced Harry and Callie, and work began. They

sat on the deck, and Harry went over a check list of concert details. Callie was relieved to find they had covered everything.

"Shall we go to Collett's for dinner?" Morgan suggested.

But before they drove into Highridge, Harry insisted on seeing the concert location.

"Where are the concession areas?" he asked.

"We hadn't planned any," Callie said. "It's sort of a picnic atmosphere. People can bring in coolers."

"Just the same, we need to sell drinks. People get hot, faint— we've got to have something to keep that from happening," he said in his gruff way. "We'll get some concessions set up tomorrow. You can make a mint on soda pop. Get it in canisters; sell only two kinds. Make it easy on yourself."

"Okay," Callie said. "We'll work on that tomorrow."

Dinner at Collett's was a noisy affair. On their previous dinner there, people had left Morgan alone, but now the summer was in full swing, and Trey was here for a concert. His name was the buzz word, and the teens swarmed him for autographs.

"Sorry about that," he said when they were safely back in the car. "Normally that doesn't happen here. A few might approach me, like at Murphy's a couple of weeks ago, but not the mob scene."

"Morgan, it's the concert, isn't it?" Callie asked. "It has them seeing you in a different way."

"It'll calm down after it's over. You'll see. In the meantime, we'd better order pizza delivery." He laughed. "Speaking of food, would you mind stopping by the Barbecue Shack? They're catering tomorrow night's dinner."

"That's fine," Harry said. "Callie and I can visit in the car while you run in." As soon as the two of them were alone in the car he started, "So, Callie, what did you think of the tabloid spread?"

"Not much. Do you think the publicity helped Morgan?"

"A picture is always publicity. I just got figures for last week, and album sales jumped twenty percent."

"Can't fight numbers, we like to say in my business."

Harry leaned toward the front seat. "Marriage used to kill a singer, saleswise. These days it's not so bad. Marriage can increase a star's popularity, make him seem more human."

"Oh," Callie said, not knowing where this discussion was leading.

"So, if Trey was to settle down, it wouldn't be the end of his career."

"And it wouldn't hurt his other life, his corporate image, at all, would it?"

"You're pretty sharp, Callie. You know this concert is costing Trey a bundle. Musicians to pay and all."

"I know. But it's for a good cause."

Harry looked her straight in the eye. "Yeah, I guess you're a good cause."

Morgan opened the door and slid inside. "All done. Don't have that to deal with tomorrow."

❧

Callie was glad she'd arranged for Friday off. She spent most of the day with Harry while Morgan and the musicians practiced. "You're a hard taskmaster, Harry," she told him after they'd arranged for soda wagons to be delivered to Dick Menner's farm by ten the next day. They had to be brought over from Asheville.

"Everything has to be in place by four," Harry said. "The place could be full by then. Carnival seating means they'll be early for the best seats—or best plot of ground, in this case."

"But they'll be sitting in the sun."

"Won't matter. You'll see."

Harry excused himself to talk to the electricians who had brought temporary power from the closest electric poles to the make-shift stage. Two flat bed trucks were parked side by side with lumber nailed over the crack between them. "Can't have a musician falling through," Harry had said.

Church members worked Friday afternoon, stringing temporary wire as a fence. Of course, people could duck through if they wanted, but the wire was to keep order.

"We've got a problem, Callie," Marilyn told her that evening when Callie arrived at Morgan's for barbecue with the band. "I went to all of our locations in every small town and Asheville. I've deposited the money in the church account."

"And the extra tickets?"

"There are no extra tickets. All locations are sold out."

"But we printed two thousand tickets!"

"Correction. I had another thousand printed on Wednesday. You were so busy, I didn't check with you. They sold in two days."

"Three thousand. That's forty-five thousand dollars."

"Minus about a hundred tickets that we gave away for equipment rentals and publicity."

"What are we going to do?" Callie asked, her eyes wide.

"We're going to entertain them." Morgan had walked up behind her and put his hand on her shoulder.

"But where do we put three thousand people?"

"Plus those who buy admission at the gate?" Marilyn inserted.

"There will be room," Morgan assured them. "It's a big field."

There was room, but only because the church members took down the wire and let the crowd spread out. Over five thousand people poured onto Dick Menner's farm. The first arrived at eight o'clock Saturday morning. By noon when the church crew was setting up the drink wagons, several hundred people had staked their claims on prime locations.

Cameras had been set up in three places. "You never know

when the energy of a concert is exactly what you need in a video," Harry said. "We tape every song he sings, no matter where."

"Good thing we didn't advertise in Atlanta," Marilyn said. "We couldn't handle the crowd. Trey's largest audience was a hundred thousand in L.A."

Callie called and ordered more soda canisters and cups. Joe Lowery picked them up for her. Dick Menner opened the gate for parking in another field and another and still another.

At six o'clock the band members arrived and plugged in their instruments. They tuned up and played a few bars of several popular songs. The crowd noise heightened. Keyed up teens stood on their blankets and swayed with the music.

Callie, who had been on her feet all day, walked slowly to Dick Menner's house, a half mile down the road. Morgan wanted her with him when he arrived at the concert.

Because there was no curtain, Harry had demanded that Morgan be brought to the stage from the back of the field. A four-wheel vehicle would take the long way around the farm so that he could make an entrance.

"Absolutely necessary," Harry had said. "You'd have a riot on your hands if Trey walked through that crowd."

The band members honked as they turned into Menner's drive. They were to wait at the farmhouse until time to go on stage. They were already settled inside by the time Callie walked into the living room. She glanced around.

"Where's Morgan?" she asked one of the musicians.

"He got a phone call as we were leaving his place. He said something about helping Dinah, but he'd be here on time."

"Dinah? You mean Dianne?"

"Yeah, that's it. He'll be here."

Callie glanced at her watch. Six-thirty.

fifteen

At first Morgan hadn't recognize the agitated female voice on the other end of the line.

"Slow down, take a deep breath and start over. I can't understand you," he said.

"Mom, Dad, and P.J. have been in a wreck. I need a ride to the hospital." She was breathless and ran her words together, but he recognized Dianne's voice.

"All right. I'll be right there," he said. "Do you know how badly they're hurt?"

"No. The hospital just called and said they were there and there had been an accident. All the others in my family have their cars at your concert."

"Stay calm. I'll be right there." He turned to one of the musicians. "Go on without me. I need to help Dianne. Tell Callie I'll be there on time."

He picked up Dianne, who jabbered the whole way into Highridge, her voice so choked with tears that he couldn't understand her words. Obviously, she didn't handle emergencies well. He wasn't sure why he was being so kind to Dianne, since he was still angry with her for her treatment of Callie, but he liked her family and couldn't be unkind to someone in need.

"This is Dianne Prescott," he told the nurse at the desk. "Some members of her family were in a car accident."

"Yes," the nurse answered, consulting a clipboard in front of her. She looked up at Morgan again. "Aren't you Trey?" she asked breathlessly.

Morgan nodded. "The Prescotts?" he reminded her.

"In the first cubicle. This way." She walked toward a hallway with the wall on one side and lined with curtains on the other. Some of the curtains were open, but the first two were pulled closed.

Morgan and Dianne followed her. The nurse drew back the first curtain and let them pass. Cooper Prescott was sitting on a chair, looking pale, but other than that without any visible injuries. Elizabeth Prescott was stretched out on the table, her right arm and right leg in splints. A doctor was examining her ribs and a nurse was checking the IV that ran into her left arm.

"Cooper, what's the situation?" Morgan asked quietly. Dianne had rushed to her mother's side and was in tears again.

The older man seemed in shock, as if he was looking at Morgan and yet not seeing him. "Elizabeth's hurt," he said in a strained voice. "I swerved to miss a dog and now Elizabeth's hurt."

"Doctor?" Morgan turned his attention to the young man in the white coat.

"She has a broken arm, broken leg, and a few bruised ribs. The leg has been shattered below the knee and will require surgery. He," he nodded at Cooper Prescott, "has a few bruises, but seems okay."

"He had a serious heart attack a few years ago," Morgan said.

"Thanks. He didn't mention that." The doctor turned to the nurse. "Have Carlton bring in the EKG and let's monitor him until the stress situation passes."

"What about their son?" Morgan asked.

"He's in x-ray. He hit the dashboard."

"Trey," the nurse with the clipboard said. "I'll show you where you can wait." She led the way out of the curtained area. Morgan followed and glanced at his watch. Quarter to seven.

"Don't worry," the nurse added. "They'll do everything they can for Phillip."

Morgan nodded at her, then did a double take. "What did you call him?"

The nurse glanced quickly at her clipboard. "Phillip. Phillip James Prescott."

P.J. Prescott was Phillip James.

"Could I see that?" Morgan asked and reached for the clipboard.

"Oh, I couldn't, Trey," the nurse protested.

"I just need to know his age," he said. "I thought it would be on there."

She consulted the sheet. "He's forty-three."

Morgan nodded. The age was right. He remembered that Jerry and P.J. were much older than Dianne and her sister. P.J. was tall, and he had dark hair.

"You can sit here and wait." She waved to a wide spot in the hall that held a few vinyl-covered chairs. "I'll come get you as soon as they get him to a room."

Morgan sat down for a few minutes, then strode back to the curtained area. Dianne still stood by her mother's side. Cooper was in the next cubicle, fastened to a heart monitor.

"Are you doing all right?" Morgan asked the older man.

"I'm all right. Elizabeth's hurt." Cooper Prescott looked at Morgan through green eyes that rivaled the color of Callie's. Why hadn't Morgan noticed that before?

He wandered back to the waiting area. He couldn't wait much longer to see how P.J. was. Callie would wonder what had happened to him. From the hospital to the Menner farm was at least twelve miles. With the curvy roads, he would need nearly half an hour to get there. He would wait until seven-fifteen to find out about P.J.'s injuries, but then he would have to leave.

He paced the hallway, checking periodically on Cooper. Elizabeth was taken to an operating room to cast her leg and arm.

Finally the nurse came back two steps ahead of a doctor. "Trey, this is Dr. Williams."

"Phillip has a broken nose, and his jaw is broken in two places. We're preparing to wire his mouth shut."

"So his injuries aren't life-threatening?"

"No. He'll take awhile to mend, but he'll be fine. He'll breath through a trachea tube while his nose is healing, probably three days or so. And he'll be on a liquid diet for six weeks. But, he'll be all right. I'll check with you after the operation."

"Thanks," Morgan called to the doctor's retreating back.

Morgan glanced at his watch again. Seven-twenty. He told Dianne what he'd learned and that he'd tell her family after the concert. Then he ran for his car.

He drove as fast as was safe around the hairpin curves out of Highridge. By the time he approached the turnoff for the Menner farm, it was ten minutes before eight.

&

Callie paced the living room floor. The musicians had already left for the concert field. Dick Menner had driven them the back way in the Jeep.

"Where is he, Harry?"

"He'll be here. Probably caught in traffic." Harry's voice was gruffer than normal, even though he was offering her some encouragement.

"He hates performing live," Callie said, wringing her hands.

"Tell me something I don't know," Harry barked. "Don't worry," he added in a less harsh voice, "he wouldn't let you down."

God, bring him here safely, Callie silently prayed. She went out on the front porch and looked down the road. Cars were still being directed onto the parking lot fields. She walked down to the drive, then back to the porch. She glanced at her watch. Five minutes until eight.

Car lights approached. Callie watched Dick Menner park the Jeep.

"Any word?" he asked.

"No," Callie said, just as another car passed the parking fields. She watched as Morgan turned in the drive. Relief left her limp.

"Where have you been?" she cried as she rushed to his side.

He explained about the wreck as they climbed in the back seat of the Jeep.

At the stroke of eight, the Jeep's headlights shone as it made its way through the back fields toward the stage.

"Are you nervous?" Callie asked Morgan.

"Petrified."

"Have you gone over the words? Have you asked for God's help?" She held his hand and he squeezed hers tightly.

"Over and over on both counts."

"He'll help you," she said and prayed silently for Morgan. She had seen the crowd; he had not. There was no way in the world that she would be able to say a word, let alone sing, in front of that many people.

They sat in the Jeep, their heads bowed together, then Morgan opened his door. "Let's do it," he said to Harry, who was already standing behind the truck beds.

At Harry's signal, the band members climbed on stage and picked up their instruments. Morgan and Callie stood hidden behind the Jeep. As soon as the musicians began a low melody,

Morgan kissed Callie and walked to the back of the make-shift stage, where steps had been erected.

"Ladies and gentlemen, please welcome Trey," Harry shouted into a mike.

Morgan bounded up the steps. The screams and applause were deafening. Trey took his place at the piano that sat in center stage and immediately launched into one of his number one hits from a few years earlier. He'd sung half of it before the crowd quieted down to listen. At the end of the song, he bowed amid screams and squeals.

Callie stood behind the stage and listened as he sang a slow ballad. The crowd quieted down but erupted again when he finished the song. For the next hour and a half, the high tension between performer and audience never diminished.

Dusk had fallen. The plan had been to end the performance before it got pitch black. Temporary lights had been attached to the few permanent electric poles that marched across Menner's field, but the weak beams didn't light the parking lots, and the new moon would give little light. Since the crowd was used to the lights only on the stage, Callie hoped they would be able to see well enough to clear the fields after Morgan finished.

"This is a new song that's going on my next album," Trey was telling the crowd. "I hope you like it. It's about this area and a very special woman."

Another musician took Morgan's place at the piano, while Morgan walked to the front of the stage with a hand mike. The band struck up a chord and Morgan crooned:

"Where the Blue Ridge meets the Smokies
Lies the place that I love best.
Where the deep sky meets the mountain peaks
 And the tall trees give me rest,
God smiled on this sweet country,

For here I met my Callie.
My Callie. Oh, sweet Callie,
I love you, my sweet Callie. . ."

Callie's hand flew to her open mouth. What was he saying? He had written the song for her!

"He wants you on stage," Harry growled at her. "Go." He pushed her up the steps.

She stumbled at the top for there was no hand rail and the lights blinded her, but she regained her balance and walked toward Morgan. He had turned and stretched out his hand to her. She took it and stood beside him as he sang, "Share my North Carolina home? My Callie, oh, my Callie, will you share my mountain home?"

Callie looked into the eyes staring into hers. The two of them were in a world of their own, even though over five thousand people watched them, spellbound.

"Will you marry me?" he whispered, but his soft words carried over the North Carolina field and five thousand people held their breaths, waiting for her answer.

"Yes," Callie said, and a cheer erupted from the crowd. Morgan kissed her and catcalls echoed off the mountains.

When the screams and shouts died down, Morgan spoke. "This concert tonight is to raise money for Callie's church, which is in bad need of repair. Lots of folks have worked hard to make sure this performance went off all right. Help them out by picking up all the cups and litter and taking them with you. Could we pick up right now before our last song?"

He laid down the mike and picked up a cup he'd been drinking from and handed it to Callie. She collected paper cups from the other musicians, then sat down on the edge of the stage. The audience buzzed as en masse they picked up the litter that had accumulated during the day.

As soon as the noise died down and people had resumed

their seats on blankets and lawn chairs, Morgan picked up the mike again.

"I'd like to close with a song that's always been special to me. If you listen to the words, you'll understand the faith I've built my life on. When I finish, if you really liked the concert, would you be silent for a moment and then leave quietly?"

He nodded to the band, and they began the sweet strains of "Amazing Grace." In his strong tenor voice, Morgan sang with an emotion that touched Callie's heart.

With the last note, the stage lights flicked off, except for one dim spotlight on Morgan. He stood still, his head bowed. No one moved. No one spoke. For five minutes the silent ovation continued. Then the few lights on the electric poles came on, and the spotlight on Morgan was turned off.

sixteen

"I've never seen anything like it," Harry said back at Morgan's house on Regal Mountain. "Not a peep the whole time they were loading their cars."

The band and Callie, Grandma, Joe, Morgan's family, Marilyn, and Robert had returned to celebrate the fund-raiser. Over seventy-five thousand dollars had been raised to restore the old church.

"Sakes alive, I never thought we'd raise this much money," Grandma said when Marilyn finished with the last of the preliminary figures.

"Of course, we've got a few more bills coming in," Marilyn said. "The electricians and the drink wagons. Wow, did drinks bring in the money."

"We're paying the musicians, too," Callie said. She'd already discussed it with the committee, and they had unanimously agreed that Morgan shouldn't pay the expenses of his band.

"Oh, we've had a meeting, and we decided we'd donate our time," said one of the musicians. "That was quite a concert. We're all glad to have been a part of it."

Grandma shook each musician's hand and thanked them all.

"What I've never seen, and I've been to a lot of concerts," Robert said, "was the way the place was cleaned up. There wasn't an empty cup on that field. That was a stroke of genius, Morgan."

Morgan smiled. "I didn't want Callie up until three in the

162

morning cleaning that place up."

"Speaking of time," Grandma said. "It's past my bedtime now. You want to take me home, Callie?"

Callie glanced at Morgan. She had left her pickup parked at Menner's farm house, and she and Grandma had ridden to the mountain in Morgan's van.

"I'll take you home, Grandma," Joe offered.

"I'll be home soon," Callie called to their retreating backs.

"They're night owls," Morgan said, nodding at the musicians. "Why don't we go get your truck, Callie?"

"I think the newly engaged couple wants to be alone," one of the musicians said. The others teased them, too, as Morgan and Callie slipped out the kitchen door to the garage.

Instead of driving on down the road to Menner's house, Morgan drove into the concert field. He helped Callie out of the van and held her hand as they walked to where the two flat bed trucks were still parked. The headlights from the van illuminated the steps and they climbed up and sat down on the stage with their feet dangling over the side. Morgan put his arm around her.

"Callie, I didn't mean to propose to you tonight," Morgan said softly.

Callie's heart stopped. He'd been moved by the moment, and the whole thing had been a mistake?

"I intended to propose when it was just the two of us, without an audience. But it just came out of me. I love you, and I couldn't hold it in any longer. I don't even have a ring yet. I hope you don't mind that so many people witnessed our private moment."

"I wasn't aware of anyone else. Just you. It was a perfect night." She traced his cheek with her fingers. "I love you, Morgan."

He kissed her softly and held her close, then let out a long sigh. "I may have found your father," he blurted. She pulled back from him. "Sorry, I didn't mean to say it so abruptly. I just don't want any secrets between us. Tomorrow we'll go to the hospital to see him."

"Hospital? Where? Is he ill?"

"He's in Highridge. He was in a car wreck, but he's going to be okay."

"A wreck?" Callie's mind processed that fact. "P.J. Prescott is my father?" She felt as if someone had punched her in the stomach.

"His name is Phillip James. I don't know that he's your father, but everything points to it. Right now all his family's at the hospital, so it would be better if we wait until tomorrow to see him. Callie, I don't know if his family will accept you."

"It doesn't matter," she said, but tears formed in her eyes. "I have you. You and Grandma are my family. And Vic and Adam and their kids and Dorothy."

"And we'll have our own children, too," he promised and kissed the tears that flowed down her cheeks.

ஐ

Callie was ready when Morgan picked her up at seven-thirty the next morning. He had suggested the early visit to the hospital with hopes that they could discover the truth and Callie could have a little time to recover before Sunday School. If she was terribly upset, the Sunday School meeting would lift her spirits, as a celebration covered-dish picnic was scheduled after the service.

The hospital staff flitted around with the after breakfast routine. Several nurses smiled at Morgan and Callie, and one gave them directions to P.J.'s room.

They walked into P.J.'s room unannounced. It was empty.

"He went to his mother's room," a nurse said from the

doorway. "Room one-fourteen. He wasn't content until he could see for himself how she was."

They walked down the hall and found the room. Callie held tightly to Morgan's hand. He squeezed her fingers as they walked through the doorway.

Elizabeth Prescott lay in a hospital bed looking old and haggard, her immaculately applied makeup missing. Her arm and leg were in casts. P.J. sat in a wheelchair, his face badly swollen, a pad of paper and a pencil on his lap, an IV pole beside him.

"Good morning, Elizabeth," Morgan said. "You remember Callie Duncan?"

Something akin to fear lurked in the older woman's eyes. "What do you want?" she asked.

"We wanted to talk to P.J.," Morgan answered.

"He can't talk. He had a tracheostomy. We're both in pain. Could you come another day, Trey?" She didn't include Callie in the invitation.

P.J. scribbled on his pad and held it up.

"Are you related to Daisy Duncan? You look like her," Morgan read. "Yes," he said to P.J. "Callie's her daughter."

Elizabeth Prescott moaned. P.J. paid no attention but wrote another note. "Where are Daisy and Sam?" Morgan read. "I don't know Sam," he told P.J. "Daisy died twenty-three years ago giving birth to Callie."

P.J.'s eyes widened and he slowly shook his head.

"You didn't know?" Morgan asked.

He shook his head no.

"Please go," Elizabeth said. "We need our rest."

Callie stepped forward. "Before she died she called out, 'Phillip, Phillip.' Are you that Phillip?"

P.J. nodded yes and scribbled on the pad. "I loved her. She married Sam," Callie read. "No," she said to him, "she didn't marry any Sam. She wrote to you that she was pregnant, but you never answered her letter."

P.J. shook his head, then grabbed it with his hands, as if he had hurt himself.

"You didn't know?" Callie asked.

He shook his head again.

"But *you* did, didn't you?" Morgan asked Elizabeth.

"I read that letter and burned it," she spat out. "And I'd do it again. P.J.'s too good to associate with ignorant mountain people, and he sure didn't need a brat around to spoil his life."

"He loved my mother. Did you really believe it was your choice to make? Why did you tell P.J. that my mother had married Sam?" Callie was guessing on that score, but it seemed very possible that Mrs. Prescott had meddled there, too.

"He moped around once we left Regal Mountain. I told him she called and said she was marrying somebody named Sam. Once he knew she'd dumped him, he got over her, even though he started staying at college through the summers and wouldn't come back to Regal with us. He met his wife and got married. Now that you know, get out of my room. Stay out of our lives."

"All right," Callie paused before she added, "Grandmother."

P.J. shook his head and reached for Callie. Tears rolled down his cheeks. Callie took his hand. "She loved you to the end," she said and kissed his swollen face.

"We'll come back later this afternoon, P.J.," Morgan said. "Do you want to be wheeled back to your room?"

He nodded.

"Don't go, P.J.," his mother called, but P.J. wouldn't turn around to look at her.

"Good-bye, Grandmother," Callie said and pushed the IV

stand while Morgan pushed P.J.'s chair.

They delivered P.J. to his room and Morgan helped him back into the hospital bed.

"We'll be back," Callie said. "Do you want us to come?"

P.J. nodded. "Want to know you," he wrote on the pad.

Callie smiled and nodded. "I'll be back."

She held on tight to Morgan's hand as they walked out of the hospital; as soon as they were in his car, she burst into tears. Morgan held her while she sobbed. A few minutes later she dried her eyes with his handkerchief.

"Do you intend to give her another chance?"

"No. I'll see P.J., but not her. She destroyed my mother. That's selfish of me, isn't it?"

"It's very human, but you may change your mind. I imagine your mother would want you to know your father. And God will help you forgive the Prescotts."

Morgan chuckled and Callie looked at him as if he'd gone mad. "There's a funny side to this, Callie. Dianne is going to be my aunt by marriage."

With the emotional trauma of finding her father and being tossed out by her grandmother, Callie wanted to cry again, but instead, she laughed along with Morgan.

"Let's get to the Sunday School meeting. We have a lot to celebrate," Morgan said. "Time and prayer will straighten out our relationship with that family, but right now I want to concentrate on our own lives. We need to set a date for our wedding."

epilogue

Callie had wanted Grandma to walk her down the aisle, but Grandma said it wasn't fitting. Although Callie was on good terms now with her father, she didn't think he should be the one to give her away since he hadn't raised her. So she decided to walk down the aisle alone. What really mattered was that Morgan would be at the other end.

Although the wedding had been planned for Sunday afternoon, it had been moved up to midnight Friday to avoid a media circus. Harry had told Morgan that the press coverage would be good for his image, but Morgan had said that though his proposal was public, his wedding would be a private affair. Callie had known it would be at midnight, but the few guests had been called at five that afternoon and told of the change of plans. The air of secrecy had added more excitement to the already keyed-up Callie.

The long summer had gone, and with the last leaves of autumn, renovations on the church had been completed. Callie and Grandma had made several trips to Atlanta to visit Morgan, to see what his life was like. Grandma had insisted that Callie know the winter side of a summer person, and Callie had delighted in her new knowledge of Morgan. She'd seen him as a singer and as a business executive, but knew that his Christian heart controlled both professions.

Work continued on the highest peak of Eagle Mountain on Morgan's and Callie's summer home. Grandma had given them the land as a wedding present, but declined to live with them when it was finished.

"My place is in the valley," she said. "At the foot of Eagle, where I've spent my life."

"But you'll visit us in Atlanta, won't you?" Callie had asked. "The winters get pretty cold in the mountains."

"I might consider it my winter home," Grandma had said and chuckled.

A knock on the van door arrested Callie's thoughts. Since there was no place to change inside the church, Grandma and Callie had waited in the van for their entrance.

"It's time." Marilyn stuck her head inside the side door.

"Are they here?" Callie asked.

"The whole Prescott clan," Marilyn said.

"Okay. Give me two minutes."

Marilyn ducked out, leaving Callie alone with Grandma.

"Thank you, Grandma, for all you've done for me."

"Why, child, it's been my pleasure."

"And please be nice to the Prescotts. I know this is awkward, but I wanted to make a gesture of forgiveness."

"Without Phillip, I wouldn't have had you," Grandma said. With a lace handkerchief, she wiped a tear from her eye. "My Daisy made a mistake—but God always seems to take our mistakes and turn them to joy. If He can forgive, then I reckon I can too."

Callie flung her arms around Grandma and whispered, "No matter what my relationship with them evolves to, it has nothing to do with my love for you."

"I know that, Callie Sue. Morgan told me love is the only thing you can divide and it doesn't get smaller. And I believe it. Now, don't you start cryin'. He's waitin' for you in there. Let's go."

Callie followed Grandma out of the van into the night. A full moon illuminated the church yard, and lights from the church beckoned them forward. At the door, Grandma arranged Callie's wedding gown that she had sewn, then disappeared inside.

Callie waited in the darkness alone until the door swung open. In the flickering candlelight, she could see Morgan. He was waiting for her.

A Letter To Our Readers

Dear Reader:

In order that we might better contribute to your reading enjoyment, we would appreciate your taking a few minutes to respond to the following questions. When completed, please return to the following:

Rebecca Germany, Editor
Heartsong Presents
P.O. Box 719
Uhrichsville, Ohio 44683

1. Did you enjoy reading *Callie's Mountain*?
   ❑ Very much. I would like to see more books
      by this author!
   ❑ Moderately
      I would have enjoyed it more if _____ .

   _____

2. Are you a member of *Heartsong Presents*? Yes No
   If no, where did you purchase this book? _____

   _____

3. What influenced your decision to purchase this
   book? (Check those that apply.)

   ❑ Cover   ❑ Back cover copy

   ❑ Title   ❑ Friends

   ❑ Publicity   ❑ Other _____

4. On a scale from 1 (poor) to 10 (superior), please rate the following elements.

    ___Heroine   ___Plot

    ___Hero   ___Inspirational theme

    ___Setting   ___Secondary characters

5. What settings would you like to see covered in *Heartsong Presents* books?

    _____

    _____

6. What are some inspirational themes you would like to see treated in future books?_____

    _____

    _____

7. Would you be interested in reading other *Heartsong Presents* titles?   ❏ Yes   ❏ No

8. Please check your age range:
❏ Under 18   ❏ 18-24   ❏ 25-34
❏ 35-45   ❏ 46-55   ❏ Over 55

9. How many hours per week do you read? ———

Name _____

Occupation _____

Address _____

City _____ State _____ Zip _____

Veda Boyd Jones

___*Gentle Persuasion*—Dallas Stone, former major league pitcher, represents everything Julie Russell despises, yet she is strangely drawn to him. Can gentle persuasion help both Julie and Dallas find room for each other's gifts? HP21 $2.95

____*Under a Texas Sky*—Abby Kane is caught in a stampede of emotions when her hometown is selected as the location for an upcoming movie. Called in to assist screenwriter Rob Vincent, Abby is soon captivated by both the process of making movies and the man himself. HP34 $2.95

___*The Governor's Daughter*—Landon shares Gayle's faith in God and her fascination with politics, but Gayle resists his attempts to discover her true identity. Hurt once already, she has no desire to be loved only as the governor's daughter. HP46 $2.95

___*A Sign of Love*—Andrea Cooper is comfortable with her life as a high school history teacher, president of the local historical preservation society, and active church member. Comfortable, that is, until Grant Logan bursts into her life. HP78 $2.95

....Hearts ♥ng.....

..... Presents ....

Great Inspirational Romance at a Great Price!

Heartsong Presents books are inspirational romances in contemporary and historical settings, designed to give you an enjoyable, spirit-lifting reading experience. You can choose from 112 wonderfully written titles from some of today's best authors like Colleen L. Reece, Brenda Bancroft, Janelle Jamison, and many others.

When ordering quantities less than twelve, above titles are $2.95 each.

SEND TO: Heartsong Presents Reader's Service
P.O. Box 719, Uhrichsville, Ohio 44683

Please send me the items checked above. I am enclosing $_____
(please add $1.00 to cover postage per order. OH add 6.25% tax. NJ
add 6%.). Send check or money order, no cash or C.O.D.s, please.
To place a credit card order, call 1-800-847-8270.

NAME _____

ADDRESS _____

CITY/STATE_____ ZIP _____

HPS FEBRUARY

Hearts♥ng Presents
Love Stories Are Rated G!

That's for godly, gratifying, and of course, great! If you love a thrilling love story, but don't appreciate the sordidness of popular paperback romances, **Heartsong Presents** is for you. In fact, **Heartsong Presents** is the *only inspirational romance book club*, the only one featuring love stories where Christian faith is the primary ingredient in a marriage relationship.

Sign up today to receive your first set of four, never before published Christian romances. Send no money now; you will receive a bill with the first shipment. You may cancel at any time without obligation, and if you aren't completely satisfied with any selection, you may return the books for an immediate refund!

Imagine. . .four new romances every month—two historical, two contemporary—with men and women like you who long to meet the one God has chosen as the love of their lives. . .all for the low price of $9.97 postpaid.

To join, simply complete the coupon below and mail to the address provided. **Heartsong Presents** romances are rated G for another reason: They'll arrive *Godspeed!*